XOXX I LOVE YOU MORE

JULIE CAPULET

Book 2 in the I Love You Series

Our connection began with an intense lust and a white-hot obsession. Then it deepened into an all-encompassing love affair that awes us both. But when Rafe's jealousy reaches fever-pitch, I have no choice but to run. As it turns out, Rafe's brother Max is my port in the storm...

Will Max cross a line? And can I forgive Rafe for loving me too much?

Our tangled web only gets more complicated when I return to Downtown to start my new job. Rafe has to somehow figure out how to balance his love with his overprotective urges. But will an ex from Rafe's past and a colleague who has no idea what Rafe and his possessiveness are capable of be enough to drive us apart again?

Or are we as destined to be together as our hearts insist?

Find out in XOXX I Love You More, the explosive conclusion to the I Love You series.

*This is the second book of a duet. It is recommended that

you read the first book, <u>XOXO I Love You</u>, before reading this one.

1

To set the record straight, I'm not usually the kind of person who wakes up in a total stranger's apartment, wearing a rain-soaked shred of a very-tight dress, drunk, lost, broke and as helpless as a girl can pretty much be. I've spent my entire life training myself to be an independent twenty-first century woman who's fully prepared to take the world by storm—and avoiding situations exactly like the one I'm in right now.

Things don't always turn out the way you wish they would.

I'm regaining consciousness after a record-breaking meltdown that I'm only now beginning to fully recall. And I'm starting to regret...a lot of things. One, letting myself get carried away by a hurricane of lust and a fairy tale of a love affair that promised from the very first second I saw him that it was way too good to be true. Two, possibly overreacting by chugging at least twice as much champagne as a reasonable person ever would. Three, not bringing my phone so I could at least call my best friend Tess to come and pick me up.

As it is, I'm struggling even to open my eyes. My awareness feels overwhelmed by a thick, invisible fog.

Someone is undressing me, with warm, strong hands. Peeling my wet dress away from my cold skin.

Who?

"Lexi, you need to get these wet clothes off. You're soaked to the skin and you're cold. Hold still." I can't do anything *but* hold still. My body feels like it's made of lead. His voice sounds familiar, but I can't place it. "I'm going to put this robe on you and wrap you in my duvet. You need to get warm."

It takes a gargantuan amount of effort, but I finally do it. I manage to open my eyes enough to see who's here with me. As soon as I see his face, it all comes rushing back.

It's Max.

Max Black.

Rafe's brother.

Rafe, my intense, beautiful lover—and boss, possibly, although I can't remember how we left it. I'd gone to the job interview at his company, Downtown, and I'd literally been swept away by a rush of lust and attraction neither of us had been able to control. It had been crazy. Wild. And totally unlike me. I'd fallen for him from that very first second. You read about things like that happening to people, love at first sight and all that, but you never expect it to happen to *you*. I'd spent the past two weeks with him, at his beach estate in Kauai, surfing, falling deeply in love with him, telling him things I've never told anyone, and having sex with him practically every hour of the day and night, in his bed, on his private beach, on his super-yacht, on his jet...

But then, as soon as we arrived back in L.A., he'd proceeded to *lock me in his bedroom* before leaving me to go to his office.

It was one of those things—actually, the *one* thing—I just really can't handle. A hangover from a mess of a child-hood I prefer not to think about.

I'd escaped. And I'd run from him. I remember every-thing now.

I left him.

I've left Rafe.

Max's hands are on my body as he peels off my skimpy outfit. Slowly. Carefully.

Am I wearing anything underneath my dress? A lacy bra and a tiny pair of La Perla panties. Rafe bought them for me, of course, as he'd bought me practically everything else I own, that day he took me shopping on Rodeo Drive.

I can't even speak. His hands are so insistent...and so *warm*.

I'm shivering. I sigh as his hands touch me, I'm not sure

why. It feels good to have the cold layer taken off. I can hear his breathing, like it's heavier than normal. He's pulling the dress away from my shoulders, adjusting me so he can pull the wet fabric away from my skin.

Max doesn't try to take off more than my dress, and I'm relieved by this.

He's rubbing me with something soft. A towel. He's drying me, and he's so, so gentle. He's muttering something under his breath. *Fucking hell. If you were anyone else's...anyone else's...keep your fucking cool, Max. Jesus H. Christ.*

My consciousness wanders for a second. My eyes once again have become too heavy to open. But then I hear him speaking in a low, soothing voice. He's talking to me. *You know that day I first met you at the restaurant, Lexi—and I know what this sounds like under the circumstances—I wanted you for myself. I did. I'm not proud of it, but I did. I wouldn't have acted on it, of course not. But Rafe knew it. There's something about the two of us, you and me, Lexi, that just...meshes. We're similar people. I don't often meet people like me, so I noticed it. I think you did, too. If you were anyone else's girl— anyone at all—I'd pick you up and carry you away with me, damn the consequences. Because it's him, I won't do what I want to do right now. I won't cross a line even though I want to cross a fucking line. So bad it hurts.*

It's hard to process the words. Maybe I'm dreaming. Maybe it *is* Rafe. Maybe I'm in his bed, wet from the shower or the beach. Maybe it's *him* who's touching me, and murmuring to me in the darkness.

But no. His voice and his indecision...it can't be Rafe. Rafe never hesitates.

Max is wrapping something around me now. Something soft. A robe. He's tying it at the waist. Then he lays me back and drapes a quilted duvet around me, tucking me in.

"There," he says, and he sounds relieved. "You're warm now. And safe. Can you open your eyes? Can you hear me, Lexi?"

It takes some effort, but I finally do it. At first everything looks murky. The room is dark, but the light from the windows casts the interior of Max's plush apartment with a low, twinkling glow.

I'm on his couch and Max is sitting next to me. He looks...big. His broad shoulders look huge and his dark hair frames his face sort of wildly. If I didn't know him, I might feel afraid of him. He definitely has the bad-boy vibe going on and I'm at his mercy. But his shadowed, stunning face looks concerned.

"Hi," I manage to say.

He stares at me for a long moment. Then he shakes his head like he's sort of exasperated with me. "*Shit,* you scared me. I'm calling a doctor."

"No." I try to sit up a little but the room spins violently, so I lay back down. My voice sounds rasped and my throat is sore. "Please. I don't need a doctor. Just a glass of water."

He goes to get one. After a minute, he comes back and helps me sit up enough to sip the cool water and swallow the two Tylenol he hands me.

"Good girl," he says, after I drink it all. "That'll help."

I look at his face...so like his brother's, yet also so *unlike* him.

I miss him.

"You passed out, do you remember?" he says.

"A little."

"You were cold. I carried you up here and put something warmer on you, so you wouldn't come down with pneumonia or something." He's justifying it, like maybe he feels guilty for taking my clothes off, but I'm glad now. I feel a little better. The haze is starting to lift at the edges.

"Thank you, Max. I feel warmer already." After a pause, I ask him quietly: "Did you call him?"

"No. Not yet." I remember pleading with him not to call Rafe. He listened, and I'm grateful. I can trust him, which means something. "I'm not going to call him until you want me to. But you know as well as I do that he'll be insane with worry right now. He might hurt himself. Not intentionally but he goes into a rage when...well, when someone he loves is threatened or lost. He reacts badly to things like that."

I close my eyes again. I don't feel up to having it out

with Rafe tonight. He'll be very intense, like he always is. All my anger has seeped out of me somewhere between bolting from Rafe's apartment and finding myself here in Max's. I could sleep for a while and insist that Rafe is kept in the dark while he meanwhile spends the night scouring the streets of L.A., desperately trying to find me. It would serve him right, maybe, after what he did.

Then again, maybe he's suffered enough. Max is right. Rafe will literally be going crazy.

I don't want him to hurt himself.

Also, against my better judgement, I *crave* him, like I've gone too long without my fix. *He's* warm, warmer than anyone I've ever met. My mouth feels strangely thirsty for him, like I miss the taste of him. I miss the haven of all that he is.

I feel a light touch on my hair and my face, and I open my eyes. Max is smoothing a strand of my hair, tucking it behind my ear in a familiar, almost absent-minded way.

This might be another reason to call Rafe. Max has acted nothing but honorably. But he's also a reckless soul. Rafe talked about it, and I can see it. The way he's looking at me now, behind the mask of his fragile self-control and his loyalty, there's something else. The thoughts flashing behind his eyes are...better left alone. I vaguely remember him saying something about carrying me away with him. And about us being similar people. It's true, for better or for worse. We are. We were targets who refused to be victims. Neither of us came away unscathed. I can admit I feel a connection to him in a way I rarely feel.

Either way, I don't really want to test him.

Or Rafe.

"What do you want me to do, Lex?"

I almost ask him to call Rafe and tell him to come tomorrow, so I can sleep for a while first. But that would never happen. I know Rafe well enough to know one thing: he won't wait. That would be like asking a herd of rampaging bulls to ignore a sea of waving red flags. "We should make sure he's okay."

My hair falls through Max's fingers as he pulls his hand away, as though realizing his mistake. He's watching my eyes. "You sure?"

I don't know why I hesitate for another few seconds. I'm scared of Rafe finding me here. I have no idea how he'll react to that. But there's nothing to react to. Max took care of me. He helped me when I needed him. "Yes."

With that, Max pulls his phone out of his pocket and calls his brother.

2

RAFE

I ALMOST DON'T ANSWER it. I don't even know if I'm capable of talking on the phone right now. But then, maybe Max can help me. Besides, we have a pact. We always answer.

"Max," I say gruffly, my gaze still fixed on the sidewalk as we drive, looking for any sign of her. White-blond hair. Suede coat. In a city of four million, she has to be somewhere. *My girl. Please, please be her.* But it never is.

"Lexi's here," he says. "At my place."

This information literally stuns me for a few seconds. "What?"

"I found her at a bar. She was a little out of it and wet from the rain. It was shaping up to be...a situation. So I brought her home."

Fuck. "Is she okay?"

"She's okay. A little out of it, but she'll be fine."

A million questions pummel through my brain like a

barrage of exploding bullets. *What happened? Did...* anything *happen? Did you touch her? What's she wearing?* I trust my brother with my life, but not much else. "Make a U-turn," I bark at my driver, giving him Max's address. "As fast as you can get us there."

Lexi is at Max's?

How? Why?

The only thing I'm certain of is the fact that I'm going to beat my brother to a fucking pulp if there's even the slightest possibility that he...no, it's too bizarre and down-right excruciating to even contemplate.

Lexi's safe, that's the main thing. She's at Max's and she's safe.

I need to get there. Now. We're not far. But traffic is heavy and we're stopped at a red light that seems to last at least a millennium.

So I jump out of the limo and start running down the street like a goddamn lunatic. I hate it when people run through the streets of L.A. Or anywhere else. But today, I don't give a flying fuck what I look like. I just need to see her. To make sure she's okay. I need to get to her before my brother's shaky-at-best scruples break down, if it's not already too late.

Zig-zagging through the crowd at high speed without fatally injuring anyone (that I know of), I run the three blocks in world-record time, possibly. I get screamed at, grabbed and even punched at one point, but I hardly notice.

The doorman of Max's building opens the door for me and it's a good thing he does. There's no telling what I'm capable of. He even says something to me. *Go right on up, Mr. Black. Your brother's expecting you.*

You're goddamn right he's expecting me. He's expecting my fucking fist to connect with his fucking face. I'm already in the open elevator, punching the button for the top floor and the apartment that *I* helped him find, secure *and* finance. A fact that never bothered me at all. Until now. Until right fucking now, as I'm about to find the only two people I really care about on the entire face of planet Earth, together. I can only hope those two people aren't going to reduce me to a shredded goddamn mess of torment when they make some twisted announcement, or admit some indiscretion that will rip my heart right out of my goddamn bloody chest.

I *deserve* it, whatever I find in Max's apartment, I know that.

All I want to do is to *see* her.

I pound on Max's door and he opens it abruptly, causing me to almost fall into the room.

I stand there, breathing heavily from my run.

It's dark in his living room. The only light comes from the glow of the city outside the expansive windows.

She's lying on the couch, covered by a thick duvet that's

been tucked around her. The silk of her hair shines like spun gold in the darkness. Her eyes are open, and the pale green hue of them catches the light. "Rafe," she says softly.

I kneel down next to her and take her cool hand. The relief I feel at that moment is indescribable. The fizzing adrenaline pumping through my system seems to transform into pure, zealous devotion. Fuck, I love her. Every cell in my body is tuned in to the perfect vision of her. My senses drink in every detail of her face as she watches my reaction to her. The flawless curve of her cheekbone. The light dusting of freckles across the bridge of her nose. Her golden hair, falling in mussed-up waves. The sound of her voice as she says my name, shooting an arrow of delight into my soul like I'm some love-struck romantic. Which I don't even mind being, not for her. Her eyes, bright and pooling with tears.

"You're here," she whispers. She sounds so tired.

"I'm here."

She reaches out to touch my hair, smoothing a strand of it out of my eyes. "You're hot," she smiles weakly.

"I ran to you. As soon as Max called."

As I say his name, I look up to see him standing there, next to me. My rage has cooled, now that I've seen her, like her presence is a calming elixir. The *only* thing that can calm me. "I found her at Jack's," Max says. "Just sitting there, alone, soaked from the rain."

I know my brother very well. He's accusing me. It's *my*

fault he found her that way. He's taken an interest in Lexi's well-being and protection, clearly, and I have no idea how far it goes, or what it means. Either way, he's right. It *is* my fault she ran. It's my fault she got caught in the rain. Alone and upset (also my fault) and maybe even scared.

"You just...ran into her?" I can't help asking the question. I'll tread carefully but the uncertainty is burning me.

"It was a coincidence," Max says, and I stop myself from breathing a sigh of pure relief. There was no prearranged meeting, no clandestine rendezvous or heartbreaking development, I can only hope. *Remain calm*, I command myself. *Everything will be fine if you keep your cool.*

"It was lucky," Lexi says, and the comment does nothing to soothe my precarious composure. "He's been so nice." *And you weren't.* I don't even know if she's thinking that. But *I* am.

"Lexi, honey," I begin. "I'm sorry. I didn't mean to scare you."

Lexi's tears well up. She tries to sit up and I help her. She seems weak and unsteady. And I can see now that she's wearing a blue bathrobe.

Max's blue bathrobe.

A shot of ice jolts through my veins but I don't immediately react. He would have given it to her, to change into. Her clothes were wet from the rain. I can see it there, the bunched-up scrap of the dress she'd been wearing, lying across the arm of a nearby chair.

My focus shifts to Lexi. She looks...sad. I want to rip out her sadness, and make it up to her. All the terrible things I've done. I'll fix everything. I'll right my wrongs and everyone else's. I'll give her everything I have, until she smiles again.

"I didn't tell you much about my past," she begins slowly.

"You don't have to, Lex. I shouldn't have—"

"I want to." She doesn't seem to mind that Max is listening, too. Some kind of trust has built up between them. There are things they have in common. Terrible things. Maybe she's taken some comfort in sharing the burden. "It was the threats. The man I told you about. It was finally going to happen, one night when my mother was asleep. He locked the door...he told me to wait. I didn't want to wait. I jumped out my window and I left. It was winter and very cold and I walked a few miles until I found a barn I could sleep in." Those green eyes are breaking my heart into tiny, shattered pieces. "I guess the sound of the lock took me back to all that... "

"You locked her in?" Max is disgusted, and I get it. He's not the only one. But he knows my history as well as his own. He knows my hang-ups are a side-effect of protecting *him* at all costs. "What the fuck, Rafe?"

Lexi defends me, of all things. "You couldn't have known that. I didn't tell you that part."

"It doesn't matter," I say. "You shouldn't *have* to tell me. I should never have done it. I just wanted to...keep you safe." It's fucked up. It *sounds* fucked up, the similarities between my behavior and some monster who wanted to possess her for his own pleasure and his own power. Exactly as I had. I've *become* one of the monsters I've been so determined to protect her from.

"It's not the same," she says. "Not at all. Not even close. Of course it isn't. But it scared me. I can't handle it. I just can't."

"Of course you can't. You shouldn't have to." I want to apologize again, but the words seem too small and too inadequate. And something occurs to me. "Where's your coat? Why weren't you wearing it?"

"I left it in a restaurant when some guy—" She stops when she notices my expression.

"What guy?"

"A guy who bought me a few drinks and let me use his phone. I ended up leaving through the back door. Through the kitchen. God, I need to call Tess. She might still be waiting there."

"You were in such a rush you forgot your coat." *I'll kill him. I'll kill all of them.*

"It doesn't matter now, Rafe. Max let me use his."

Keep your cool, Rafe. Do not go fucking ballistic.

"She was a little out of it," Max says. I don't have to ask why he didn't call me as soon as he found her. I remember what Bennett said. *She begged me not to.* I can hardly blame her. Even so, as I hold her hand and contemplate her face, I know I'll never give up trying to convince her to forgive me, even if it takes me the rest of my life to do it. "She fainted, and I brought her back here and got her out of her wet clothes so she could get warmed up."

He's pissed off, and so am I.

I'll admit I can be an overbearing, volatile, hot-headed asshole from time to time. As it happens, this is one of those times. Max found Lexi and possibly even talked her into allowing him to call me. I'll thank him for that at some point. But the only detail I can concentrate on right now is this one: *he stripped her out of her wet clothes. As she was unconscious. He's seen her practically naked. And I know what he was thinking: she's beautiful and perfect and I wish she was mine. Goddamn it!*

My nerves are shot twelve times over, and as much as I might try to cling to the last shreds of my own self-control, it's a lost cause. Very carefully, I ease my clasp from Lexi's hand. I stand up.

And I lunge at my brother.

It's definitely not the first time I've taken my frustrations out on Max and probably won't be the last. He uses me as his punching bag too sometimes, like a form of therapy, and always has. He might even be doing it now, for his own reasons. I still outweigh him, though.

He's expecting it. He *knows* he's guilty. He knows he enjoyed salivating all over my perfect girlfriend—and if she'll have me, soon-to-be-fiancée.

I get a good left hook in before he punches me in the face. We roll and growl and knock over a table. I get in a few more solid hits but Max is a scrappy fighter and we're evenly matched. And he's as fired-up as I am tonight. I get Max pinned down and get in another good shot before I feel her hand on my shoulder. *"Rafe. Stop it!"*

I freeze. Max does, too. She's too close to risk any more violence. *She* can't be harmed.

"Stop it right now, both of you." Lexi's expression is stern and her face is mind-numbingly beautiful. Like an angel, crouched there, scolding us. "Rafe, you leave Max alone. He's been only kind to me. He found me, and he helped me. He's done nothing wrong."

When Max speaks there's a sincerity in his voice that's unusual. He almost sounds like he's getting all emotional. *"Fuck*, Rafe. I *wanted* to, of course I did. But I wouldn't do that to you, even if you are a fucking bastard. She's yours, obviously. She's good for you. You deserve her. You two deserve each other." Then he adds, *"If* you can treat her right and stop doing dumb shit, for fuck's sake."

My brother, as close as we've been over the years, is not a sentimental kind of a guy. He keeps his emotions close to his chest. It's sort of a defense mechanism of his. This is the most heart-felt thing I think I've ever heard him say.

And I believe him.

Then he turns to Lexi and says, "You should forgive him. He saved me, and it wasn't easy. That's why he acts the way he does. He had to. I was a fucked-up kid who needed help. And he helped me. Every day. Every single day of my miserable fucked-up life. He never gave up on me. He *still* hasn't given up on me, and that's saying something. He's the best person I know and you should forgive him. He didn't mean to do anything wrong."

Max's words resonate in the sparked night, inking everything.

With that, Lexi kisses Max's cheek. "Thank you, Max, for saving me tonight."

Then she turns to me, and she's not crying anymore. "Rafe, can you take me home now?"

3

I use Rafe's phone to call Tess.

"I was about to call the *police*, Lexi. Where the hell are you?"

I explain everything, apologize a thousand times and assure her again that I'm okay.

"I'm still parked outside the restaurant," she says. "I've been waiting here for over an hour, Lex. Come home with me." I can tell she's worried about me. About how swept away and in-at-the-deep-end I've been. And still am. *I'm* a little worried about me, too, come to think of it. I actually consider taking her up on her offer. A few days of sleeping on Tess's couch, being *me* again and existing in my normal, regular world could be just what I need. This whole thing has been beyond intense.

I won't, though. Of course I won't. Rafe's watching me, holding my hand as he waits for me, and he's more beautiful than he's ever been. I can't expect him to be perfect. *I'm* not perfect, no one is. He's going to make mistakes sometimes and so am I. And there's something about his presence—after being apart from him for four or five hours—that's just such a relief to me, I feel overwhelmed by it. It's indescribable. And it's hard to know how to feel. "I'm going to go back to Rafe's for a while. I'm so sorry you had to wait so long, Tess. I didn't mean to worry you."

"You're worrying me *now*, Lexi. Are you sure you're not taking this whole thing way too fast?"

"Probably," I admit. "But I'll be fine. Let's do dinner tomorrow night, okay? I'll call you and we'll plan something. You could come over and we can talk."

"Yeah, that sounds good. But, Lex, are you *sure* you're okay?"

"Yes. I'm sure. Please don't worry about me, okay? How'd your meeting go?"

"Good. I landed the client. And stop trying to change the subject. You just seem...a little out of control. This whole thing has been so...*intense*, Lexi."

She doesn't know that half of it. "It's fine, Tess. I'm fine. Everything's fine."

"Just be careful, okay?"

"I will. And I'll call you tomorrow."

After we end the call, Rafe picks me up and carries me to the elevator, holding me against his chest, like I'm precious cargo. My emotions are still on overdrive and I don't know if I've completely forgiven him, but I can't help it. I weave my arms around his neck as the elevator doors close. I curl my fingers through his thick black hair. His muscles are flexed and hard. There's a bruise forming around his eye where Max punched him. He looks relieved but also sort of wild and unruly.

"I love you," I tell him, without even planning to, as I look into the depths of his dark blue eyes. I *do* love him, so much, and I want him to know that, despite everything. I know he'll try harder. The last thing I want to do is start crying again, but with Rafe, everything feels so close to the surface all the time, always ready to spill over.

"I love you more, baby. I'm sorry I scared you. I won't do it again." His voice is rasped with emotion and his eyes are bloodshot. If I didn't know better, I'd almost wonder if he was about to cry, too.

"I guess I'm pretty messed up. Maybe you'd be better off without me and all my baggage."

He spears me with a look. "I don't give a fuck what your baggage is, honey. I'm all in, baggage and all. So bring it on. There's nothing you could do that would scare me away."

He does have a knack for saying exactly what I need to hear, damn him. I pull his face to mine and kiss his lips softly. He groans, as though my kiss is breaking his heart.

"You know what I want to do with you?" he says, that dark husk in his voice unfurling something in me. "After we've worked out your schedule and you get acclimatized at Downtown, I want to take you to my Malibu estate for the weekend. Just you and me." He pauses, then adds. "If you want to."

A Hawaiian estate. A Malibu estate. He sure has a lot of *estates*. We're back to that old topic of whether he'll hire me or not, and he's relented, maybe, after his fuck-up.

Anyway, *this* is the Rafe I fell in love with. The one who asked me *if I was game* before taking control of every detail of my well-being. The one who charmed me and fixed me, on my own terms, and on his. "Sounds nice," I say. Now that Rafe and I have weathered our first fairly major storm, I feel even closer to him. I feel that rush, feeding my addiction, just being near him again.

The elevator pings and the doors slide open. I remember I'm still wearing Max's bathrobe. My arms are wrapped around Rafe's neck, my hands entwined in his hair as he carries me through the foyer of the building. I'm vaguely aware that the doorman opens the door for us, that the limo driver is already there, opening another door. Back to this, where people open doors for us, and give us everything we want. Rafe sets me down on the seat and slides in next to me. Then he settles me onto his lap with his arms wrapped around me.

"I'm going to take such good care of you," he whispers, staring into my eyes.

I kiss him again. Now that our drama is over, I feel

hungry for closeness. I'm done second-guessing whatever happened. I need him. His presence, his scent, his big, hard, warm body. The taste of his lips against mine is drugging, but he pulls back. "You're tired, sweetheart. You've been through the ringer. I want you to rest."

I scared him today and he's taking no chances with me. He promised to be careful, to make amends for his mistake. And he's right: the day has left me emotionally raw and also thankful. That he's mine, flaws, obsessions and all.

He holds his palm to my forehead. "Maybe you have a fever. I'm going to call a doctor."

"I don't need a doctor. I just want to go home."

Home.

His fingers gently smooth my hair. I can see that he likes the sound of the word. "I'll do anything for you, sweetheart. You know that, right? Do you know how much I adore you?" His voice is husky. "I hated not knowing where you were."

"I don't want to run from you, Rafe," I whisper. "I don't like being apart from you, either." It's scarily true.

"Maybe it wasn't just the lock," he says. "Maybe it's everything. I'm too over-protective, I know that. I can't seem to help myself. I love you too much." He's gazing at me and his eyes are framed by those long, thick lashes.

Rafe. My Rafe. I take his face between my hands. I feel

his torment like it's my own, deep inside my heart. "It's okay now. We're here. We're together."

"I can't lose you. I thought I'd lost you."

"You couldn't lose me if you tried," I tell him, despite everything.

"You've touched me, angel, like I've never been touched. I'm crazy in love with you. *Crazy*."

He kisses me for a long time, our bond humming and alive, deepening irrevocably.

I don't know what will happen. All I know is that Rafe is somehow shining his light into those places in my soul that have only known darkness. Whatever it costs me, I'm willing. I want to try.

I love him.

4

Rafe takes me home. To *his* home, of course. I don't analyze it. *Home*, to me, has never been a word that was all that comforting. Tonight, for some reason, it suddenly is.

He runs me a bath in his Jacuzzi tub. He feeds me until he's satisfied I've eaten enough. And he tucks me into bed, curling his big body around me to keep me warm as I sleep.

Late at night, he makes love to me, tenderly, with a passion he can never quite contain. I coerce him further. I willingly take everything he gives me. As equals. As lovers. As two damaged souls, hinged together by our jagged edges.

The next morning, at breakfast, I can't help noticing that Bennett is sporting a brand new Rolex. He serves us, then promptly disappears.

"What day is it?"

"Sunday." Rafe's phone pings, and he picks it up quickly, like he's been waiting for whatever message it's showing. "It's the front desk. I've ordered a few things."

"What things?"

"You'll see."

Rafe answers the door to the delivery person only in his jeans. He's shirtless, barefoot, he needs a shave, and his too-long hair, even though he deliberately smoothed it down a little as he went to open the door, is still a mess from bed. He tips the guy with a hundred dollar bill that was already in his pocket, then shuts the door with his foot. He's holding three large gift-wrapped boxes with two small ones stacked on top of the pile.

Rafe sets the boxes down on the table. Then he turns to me, his hands shoved into the pockets of his low-slung jeans. His darkly-tanned skin emphasizes the whiteness of his teeth as he smiles. "I, uh...bought you something," he says.

"Rafe," I scold him. *Something* is more accurately a whole *bunch* of things. He knows how I feel about him buying me gifts, but he does it anyway.

He smiles at me, almost guiltily, from under the fall of his hair. "Humor me. Please. Open the big ones first."

He brings me the biggest box.

I open it, and it's a brand new coat, identical to the one I left behind at the restaurant. "Rafe. You really didn't—"

"Open the next one." It's...*cute*—if an arrogant alpha

billionaire hunk can be described this way. It's sort of adorable, the way he seems so excited for me to open his presents.

The second box contains a new pair of Balenciaga boots, just like the ones I'd damaged walking through the pouring rain. "Thank you, Rafe."

"Open this one next." He hands me the last of the big boxes.

These gifts are so incredibly generous. It's hard not to get caught up in the moment. Inside the third box, there's a white dress made of fine, soft cotton, lacy and feminine. It's a modern take on a short, fitted peasant dress. I hold it up. "It's so pretty."

"Put it on."

He helps me shrug off the robe I'm wearing—Rafe's this time—and slips the dress over my head. It's a gorgeous piece of clothing. I slip on the boots and put on the coat.

He takes a step back and contemplates me, as though not quite satisfied. "Something's missing."

"What could possibly be missing?"

He picks up the two small boxes. One is pink and the other is blue. He holds one in each hand and stands in front of me. He's smiling but he also looks...nervous. Which isn't typical for Mr. Cocky. This gets me curious. "What are they?"

"You'll have to open them to find out." He hands me the pink box. "This one first."

Watching his face, I take the pink box. Carefully, I open it. It's a small gold old-fashioned-shaped key on a fine gold chain. I lift it by its chain from the box. "A key."

He holds it and shows me the engraving. "On this side, the code for all my doors." He turns it over. "On this side, the code for all my accounts. So you'll never be locked in or locked out. And you'll never need for anything you can't have."

I look up at him. He's a little bit blurry because of the tears. It's the nicest thing anyone has ever given me. This gift is a heavy statement. It's a promise.

"There's a credit card and a debit card in the box, too, which will be slightly more practical to carry around. They're yours, to use however you want. Both accounts are in your name and have five hundred thousand dollars loaded, but we can top them up if you need more."

What? "I don't want—

"Please. Open this one next." He holds out the small duck-egg blue box. **TIFFANY & CO.** is written across the top.

"*Rafe*," I whisper. I'm scared to open it. Tiffany & Co. *Am I ready for this?*

"I don't want you to be my assistant," he says.

A million emotions are coursing through my mind. I don't think he's firing me. His expression is too gentle for that. "What do you mean?"

"I want you to be a junior partner. I'm going to train

you to work alongside me. Since I can't bear to be without you, you might as well learn the business from the ground up. You're getting a promotion."

"Rafe. I haven't even...are you sure—"

"Yes. Now, if you would...please...open this one." *Please.* Rafe looks almost as hopeful yet scared as I feel.

I take a breath, and I open the small blue box. As I do, Rafe gets down on one knee.

Oh my god.

It's the biggest, glintiest diamond ring I've ever seen in my life. The huge rock is set on a solid white-gold band. It's...outrageously amazing. "*Rafe*," I whisper.

He takes my hand. "My beautiful Lexi, I can't breathe when you're not near me and I never want to be apart from you for as long as I live. I love you. I adore you. I promise to be the best man I can be for you. I'll make mistakes along the way, but I'm one thousand percent dedicated to making you happy. Will you let me try? Lexi, will you marry me?"

Rafe is watching my eyes, waiting for me to answer him and I can see that he's not sure if I'll say yes to him. All his arrogance and bravado is, for the moment, gone. He looks young and gorgeous and vulnerable, like whatever answer I give him will break his heart, for entirely different reasons.

This brings more tears to my eyes. It's a look of pure love. I'm well aware that I've only known Rafe Black for two weeks and two days. I know it would be much more logical to wait, and see how this relationship plays out for...a month or two or even six, before making such a life-changing decision. I know he's crazily intense, arrogant AF, and more than a little possessive. I have no doubt this is going to be one hell of a ride, but I say it anyway. I can't imagine loving anyone, ever, as much as I love this dazzling, complicated, exasperating man. "Yes."

His eyebrows lift. "Yes?"

"Yes. I'll marry you."

Rafe takes the ring out of its box and slides it onto my finger. It fits perfectly, like it belongs there. He admires it for a few seconds, then he stands up and takes me in his arms. He kisses me so tenderly, there's nothing else on this earth. Just him.

"I love you," he whispers. He's laughing lightly, like he's wildly relieved. "Thank God. I was afraid you might say no."

"When have I ever said no to you?"

"Well, I hope you don't say no to the engagement present I already bought you."

"What? Already?"

"I mean, I *hoped* you wouldn't say no. How do you feel about Porsche 918 Spyders? I can get you something else if you don't like it. Of course you'll also have your own limo and driver, even though you'll mainly be using mine because you'll be with me—"

"Rafe?"

"Yeah?

"I don't know how to drive."

He pauses, considering this. "You don't?"

"No. Remember the jet ski?"

He blinks, then he laughs again, before kissing me. Hungrily, endlessly. Somewhere in the middle of it, he says, "I'll teach you." Then he kisses me again.

He undresses me, peeling off my luxurious clothes, until I'm naked except for my brand new diamond ring. Rafe kisses his way down my body until I'm moaning for him, begging him, needing him. Until he's giving me everything he has to give.

Our attraction began with an uncontrollable lust and has grown into an all-encompassing bond that awes us both. There will be bumps along the road, I have no doubt about that.

He's given me his key and his ring. He's promised to be gentle with me, to teach me and to give me room to be myself.

I can't read the future, and I hope our love is strong enough to allow all that and to see us through.

Time will tell.

5

———————

HE LAYS NEXT TO ME, still asleep. His black hair is all askew, framing his face in silky disarray. His brawny shoulders are dark from our days in Hawaii. He's lying on his stomach, his face turned toward me, his muscular arm curled around his pillow. His face is peaceful. He looks younger in his sleep. Relaxed. That visceral, male aggression that clings to him softens when he sleeps, but the innate arrogance is somehow still there. In the curve of his mouth. In his strong features and the stripes of his eyebrows.

I watch him sleep for a few minutes, fascinated by his mesmerizing flawlessness. His only imperfection is the light bruises on his jaw and around his eye where Max punched him, already fading. The bruises, along with his too-long black hair and his deep tan, make him look more like some beefed-up gypsy pirate than ever.

I could touch him, with feather-light strokes across his

shoulders, like I often do to wake him. I could rub myself against him and kiss his perfect lips, licking him, tasting the minted, drugging flavor of him. I know he'll be instantly ready for me.

Rafe is always ready.

But today's the day I'm starting my new job.

As Rafe's assistant.

No. Not as his assistant. As a junior partner.

This whirlwind romance has landed me a drop-dead gorgeous sex-god of a fiancé. It's also placed me at the right hand of one of the most powerful CEOs in Los Angeles. He not only owns Downtown, the most successful magazine/blog/indie film production company in the country, but he also owns several investment companies, hedge funds, real estate all over the world, and who knows what else.

It's Monday morning, earlier than we usually wake. Rafe and I have become night owls. We talk late into the night, make love, watch movies—I'm teaching him about all the classic rom-coms—make love again, and fall asleep in each other's arms.

Sometimes when I stop to think about things, like now, I almost feel a sense of vertigo from the gargantuan shift my life has taken.

Two weeks.

Less than three weeks ago, I arrived in L.A. in baggy clothes, wearing thick glasses, lugging my old duffel bag around, which contained everything I owned. I'd slept on my best friend Tess's couch for a total of four nights.

Until Rafe stormed into my life like a category five hurricane and changed everything.

I look around me. The modern blinds over the windows go up and down by pushing a button on the remote control. They're half open. We're too high up, here in the penthouse, to be visible to people on the streets. Our view is of his outdoor patio area, his private pool, palm trees and the skyline down below us.

It's early October, but L.A. doesn't get cold, like it does up north. I like the heat. It makes me feel like I'm far away from the cold places I ran away from.

The quiet, expansive room hums with plush, cocooned luxury. Rafe's bed is huge, piled high with expensive cotton and silk, most of which is rumpled and twisted from our lovemaking.

Rafe teased me about being a prodigy in that particular department. Whoever thought virgins took things slow once they finally got going at the advanced age of twenty...well, they hadn't put me in a room with Rafe Black. There'd been a desperation to it I still can't explain.

He's my drug and my addiction. My devil and my saint. My strength and my weakness. With him, lines become skewed and normal considerations simply don't apply.

Beautiful, crazy Rafe. All mine.

Today, we'll spend the day together. But not like we usually do.

Today, we go to *work*.

I'm excited. And a little nervous, I'll admit. Not about the job itself, but about how we'll handle it. How *he'll* handle it, more specifically. Having to *resist,* and act like normal people and not amped-up, lust-crazed hedonists.

I'll agree to try *to employ you,* Rafe had said. *I can't guarantee that this will work for me, though. I'm too close, too deep. I need to be able to focus on my companies, without distractions. And you, my sweet Lexi, are more of a distraction than I can handle.*

We fought about it, before my meltdown. I know Rafe won't risk driving me away again. I have a ring on my finger and a key to his universe. He'll tame himself, or he'll die trying.

I hope it'll work.

And I want to be ready for it.

I get out of bed, being careful not to wake him. I need some time to psyche myself up and get ready to join the über-cool Downtown team. What will they think of me? Do they know that Rafe and I are...together? *Engaged?* Either way, they'll find out soon enough.

I can't help but remember...four of them. Max, a guy named Cole, Eric, one of Rafe's executive editors, and another guy whose name I can't remember...*who'd seen me that night at the poker table.* Rafe had put some kind of sex beads inside me and I'd had one of the most intense orgasms of my life right there at the poker table. Then again, pretty much every orgasm Rafe gives me is the most intense of my life, until the next one.

It's mortifying to think I'll be sitting across a table from them at a board meeting in a matter of hours, possibly. But hey, these things happen, right? I can't turn back time, as much as I might want to. Besides, Rafe will freak out enough for both of us, I have a feeling.

I take a shower, alone. It's been a while. He likes to shower with me.

If I'd stayed in bed, he would have woken me up like he always does. With his mouth on me, licking into me, softly opening me with his tongue, his hair silky against the sensitive skin of my thighs. Or with his cock, pressing its huge, hard heat against me as he spooned me. At first he'd just hold me. Then I'd feel him finding his way inside, barely entering me. He'd wait, pressing gently until my body began to accept him. I'd arch against him, taking more. And more. Until I became slippery enough for him to slide his massive arousal deep, and deeper, filling me, possessing me. His fingers would be everywhere, intimate and playful. Coaxing warm, blissful pleasure. His powerful hold would demand submission, but I'd make demands of my own. My own pleasure would tug at his, drawing the ecstasy out of him in clenching pulls, until he flooded me with his liquid heat. He'd stay inside me. We might sleep a little more. The next time he woke me, I might feel him at my breast, suckling lazily, feeding on me like I was offering him some kind of spiritual sustenance that was drugging to him. When we were fully sated, later, we'd get up. We'd shower together. He'd wash me and I'd wash him, my careful fingers soaping him everywhere. We'd make love again. Then we'd spend the day together, on his yacht, riding the jet ski, surfing, making love all over again. He'd cook for me. We'd go for a walk. We'd watch the sunset, then we'd do it all over again.

Today, things will be slightly closer to...reality? Normality? Nothing about my life has been remotely *normal* since Rafe walked into it.

I put on one of the many outfits he bought me. I choose a sleeveless sea-green silk tunic that matches the color of my eyes. It's fitted and simple and stylish. I brush my hair and pin it up. Gold hoop earrings, my new gold watch and my new ring are the only jewelry I own—all given to me by Rafe. I can't help wondering how much he spent on my engagement ring. It's outrageously...big. It looks, and feels, very, very expensive.

I put on some light makeup, and I walk back into the bedroom.

His eyes are open.

He rolls onto his back and slings one arm behind his head. The way he moves, even in bed, is cocky and totally self-assured. So purely Rafe.

His body is big and bronzed and hair-dusted and fully aroused.

"Lexi," he says, his lazy, sexy charisma hitting me where it always does. In the most intimate place imaginable. "Come here." He pats the bed.

I go to him and sit next to him.

His fingers entwine with mine and he plays idly with my ring, looking into my eyes. "Let's get married soon. I don't want to wait. We could do something small, at one of my—our—houses. Do you want to do it in Malibu? Or Hawaii?"

"Why do you have a house in Malibu? You live here. Do you really need two houses in the same city?"

"It's right on the water. There's a vineyard and a sandy beach. I'll show you this weekend." He laces his fingers through mine. "New York is nice this time of year, if you'd rather check out the east coast. We could see a Broadway show. Or Vermont, if you want to see the leaves. Or I have a place in Key West. Or Paris. Pick one."

"They all sound nice."

He contemplates me gently.

It's still a little overwhelming sometimes.

The choices. The luxury. The job. *The fiancé.*

"Which one would *you* choose?" I ask him.

"I really don't mind where I marry you, baby girl. As long as I do."

Here he goes again with the perfectly-placed, heartfelt

words that made me agree to marry him in the first place, even though I can't even legally drink a beer yet and I've known the man for a whopping two and a half weeks. "Malibu, then."

"We could honeymoon in Paris. You'll love Paris. I'll show you the sights and take you shopping."

"Rafe." Again with the shopping.

His slow smile just about kills me. "You weren't here, in my bed with me, where I need you," he accuses gently, that alpha glint touching his expression. "You're dressed," he adds sulkily.

"I'm starting work with you today. Remember?"

A smile plays at the corner of his mouth. Of course he remembers. He's king of the kingdom. He thinks it's funny, how eager I am.

I *am* eager, even if I'm wondering how the intensity of our...*attraction* will mesh with life amongst the cubicles. Not that Rafe ever gets near a cubicle, but still. After our orgasmic sexathon over the past few weeks, it'll be an adjustment. To be near him but not allowed to touch.

"Our first meeting doesn't start until nine," he says. "And our commute is exactly three minutes by elevator."

"It's already seven fifty-one. I think we should get started. Do I look okay?"

His dark blue eyes rove over my face, to the flattering fit of my new clothes. The smoldering glimmer makes my stomach flutter, like always. Slowly, he shakes his head.

"No?" I touch my hair.

"You don't look 'okay'. You look so fucking gorgeous it hurts. Right here," he says placing his hand on his heart. "And here," he smirks. His hand slides to his massive, engorged erection.

On any other day, I'd indulge him. I'd take his hard cock in my hands, and tease him with my mouth. Suck him slowly until he came in hot bursts.

On any other day, he'd ignore the phone calls, or turn his phone to off.

But not today. Today, there are overdue issues with his companies to attend to. One of them is an investigation into insider trading involving Max's investment group. His minions are getting impatient. And eight o'clock on Monday morning is fair game.

As if on cue, his phone rings, splicing through the quiet.

He's torn, I can see, but he picks it up and answers it gruffly.

I leave him to it. I walk into his walk-in closet, which is almost half-full of my new wardrobe. I pull on my boots. I don't need my coat, since it's L.A.—and also because we don't even have to go outside at all today if we don't want to.

We could live our whole lives in this building, safely locked away. The thought sends a ripple of unease through me, but then it fades. I have his key now.

I'm putting on some lipstick when he comes up behind me. He slides his steel-strong arms around my waist and nips at my neck. His huge, rock-hard cock presses strongly against my backside. I sometimes forget how *big* he is. How buff and hard all over. But his arms are gentle and his words are soft as he nuzzles my neck. "Are you nervous?"

"No. I'm excited."

"You'll be amazing today, honey. Don't worry about anything. I'll be right there with you. Whenever you need me."

"*Whenever* I need you?" I laugh lightly as he turns me to face him. His cock slides against my stomach and I can feel the heat of him through the thin silk of my dress.

Rafe nips the soft hollow below my ear with his teeth. "You'll have to try to resist me for five minutes," he murmurs.

"What if I can't?" I'm teasing him, and his cock rears up a little. I slide my fist gently around him, partly because I don't want him messing up my clothes. He looks like he's about to burst, already. Maybe it's the fact that he might have to *wait* that's getting him so worked up. His cock is leaking a bead of wetness.

"Everything will be fine," he says.

"Sure it will." I place my palm gently against his chest, and I can feel his heartbeat. It'll be...interesting. To see if we can behave like rational adults. We've never had to control our urges before.

"*You* will be perfect," he continues, kissing my mouth, "the star academic, the new Stanford grad with shining credentials and talent to burn. *I* will be the pinnacle of discipline and self-control. As I always have been. Before you showed up. And even when you, my sweet little ball of Kryptonite, walks into the room—or out of it—I'll make every attempt *not* to morph into a raving psychopathic lunatic."

Rafe has a few control issues. Letting me out of his sight makes him a little...manic. We're working on it. His smile is half-apologetic at the reference to his recent fuck-up.

But I've already forgiven him for all that.

He holds my face in his hands. "I'm going to *try* to behave like a reasonable, normal human being. As you know, that doesn't come particularly easily for me when it comes to you." He's sort of joking, but then his tone turns more serious. "You know I'd do anything for you, don't you, baby? None of it means anything to me anymore without you." He kisses me again, just a brush of his lips against mine. "I love you."

My hand slides up his neck, into the thick locks of his wild black hair. He has amazing hair. "I love you more."

He smiles and his eyelashes brush my cheek, his expression soft. This is *my* Rafe, the part of himself he saves just for me. "I'm afraid that's simply not possible."

"What about *this*?" I whisper, squeezing my fingers

more tightly around his cock, kissing his lips, touching my tongue to his. He tastes too good. He *feels* too good. I can always change my dress. He deepens the kiss, his tongue exploring as his fingers slip under my dress, rubbing my clit over the silk of my panties. I give him everything he wants. I gently suck his tongue into my mouth, craving him with a quiet, savage intensity.

But his phone rings again.

"Fuck," he mutters, breaking the kiss. "It's probably Max."

"You better answer it." Clearly, we'll have to wait until later.

A first.

He disengages reluctantly. His colossal hard-on is rigid and slick and hot-looking, his body as ripped and perfect as a genius's sculpture come to life.

I smooth my dress back into place. "I'll go downstairs and wait for you." I kind of want to...not show up together. Just for today.

Rafe takes a long look at me. Then he sighs and nods. "Okay. This could take a while. I'll meet you on the seventh floor. It's the corner office."

Of course. Every CEO needs at least two offices, one private one and one in the heart of the action. "Right."

It's surprisingly difficult, already, these interruptions. These small separations. "You've got the code," he adds, his eyes holding mine for a brief moment. There's a ripple of intimacy and I'm reminded of all that's happened between us.

"I'll see you soon."

"You've got a hot date tonight, by the way," he says, dark-eyed. "Be ready for me."

"I'm always ready for you, Rafey."

His eyes narrow with such smoldering lust I almost think he might lunge at me. But his phone is still ringing. He walks over to the bed, picks it up and answers it with a pissed-off growl. "Max. What the fuck's going on?"

I leave him to talk to his brother, knowing full well there might be some lingering...issues between them, closing the bedroom door behind me. Outside the wall of windows of Rafe's great room, the sky is blue and the sunny day is hazy. It's a perfect Monday morning in Los Angeles.

I take Rafe's private elevator down toward the suite of offices that are located on the fifth, sixth and seventh floors.

A young, trendy-looking receptionist sits behind the front desk, with the wall-sized print of the L.A. skyline behind her. I remember it, from the day of my interview, although it's a different receptionist. *The interview.* Was that only two weeks ago? It feels like a lifetime ago. So much has happened.

"Ms. Blondeau, nice to meet you," she says, which surprises me a little, that she knows who I am. "I'm Josie."

"Hi, Josie. Please, call me Lexi. It's nice to meet you, too."

Rafe, or someone else, must have told the Downtown staff about my new appointment as the CEO's assistant...or junior partner. They know their CEO took two weeks off for the first time ever. My ring is turned, so the skating rink of a diamond is hidden in my fist. I return her handshake with my right hand.

Josie shows me to Rafe's office. "Have a good first day," she says.

"Thank you."

His office is even bigger than the one upstairs. It's all windows, overlooking the pool, but tinted so you can't see in from the outside (I'm guessing, but I'd bet money on it. It's the kind of detail I've come to expect from Rafe). There's a desk, an area with couches and a coffee table, then a large meeting table with twelve chairs around it. No one else is here yet so I go over to the coffee station and make myself a cup.

I feel distracted. And restless. From the thought of...the way I left him.

For god's sake, Lexi. You're at work. Focus. Absolutely do not *let yourself be reminded of...how hard he was. How mouth-wateringly hot.*

"Ms. Blondeau, welcome." I jump a little, startled. A woman is standing there knocking lightly on the open door. She's probably around thirty, with a short brown bob and tortoise-shell glasses. She's smiling and attempting to control her fascination, I can see this. I guess it's a vibe I'll need to get used to. I slid my diamond back around when I made my coffee. She's staring at it now, and her eyes get wide. Then she collects herself. "I'm Claire Powell, one of the associate editors. Congratulations on getting the job as Rafe's assistant. We had about a million applications."

"Thank you, Ms. Powell."

"God, that makes me sound about a hundred years old. Please, call me Claire."

"Claire." She's nice, and I appreciate the way she's trying to put me at ease.

"I can show you around while you wait for Rafe to arrive, if you'd like."

"Thank you."

Claire gives me a quick tour, introducing me to several other staff members. All of them watch me. I have no idea how to read their reactions. I feel surprisingly unaffected, like I'm one step removed somehow, as if I've been coated with a thin veneer of power. Which is ridiculous. *I* don't have power. Over anyone. I don't even *want* power.

But I can't help the thought from creeping in...*their* mogul boss is *my* very-possessive fiancé, who will literally do anything I ask of him, and who has shared with me the most passionate, transformative, intimate experiences of my life, and his. *I can bring your CEO to his knees. I can make him come so hard with the flick of my tongue and the squeeze of my fingers that he groans like his heart's being ripped out of his chest. He belongs with me. He's mine.*

Jesus.

I've accused Rafe of being obsessive but I'm equally guilty. I don't even care at this point. I just want to see him again. I miss his black-haired, swarthy presence and the sparks in the room whenever he's near me. I'm having some crazy withdrawal symptoms, is what it boils down to.

Claire gives me a tour of the outdoor area, where a lot of people are working in the private pods and the loungers. Some people are even swimming in the pool.

Claire leads us back to Rafe's office, which is still empty. "Thanks for the tour, Claire."

"We should do lunch sometime."

"I'd love that."

"We'll set something up later," she says. "I'll see you after the meeting."

Then she leaves and I'm alone in the room. There's a stack of printed booklets that outline the agenda of the meeting we're about to have so I put one in front of each chair, just to give myself something to do.

Rafe sweeps in like a stormy-eyed, billionaire monsoon. I swear the temperature in the room spikes. His energy fills the space, crowding around me like tropical warmth. He closes the door.

He looks almost windblown, like he's been rushing. Even from across the room, I can detect his relief. *He rushed so he could see me.* A little fissure in my heart opens a fraction wider with the realization, that I'm not the only one suffering from this full-blown addiction.

Rafe is dressed in a beautifully-cut three-piece suit. He looks clean and hastily-groomed. His hair is still damp from his shower. It's been a while since I've seen him dressed up (once) and the effect shoots straight to the pit of my stomach. The combination of his wild ferocity, contained as it is in his business clothes, is sort of...ridiculously hot.

He places his leather briefcase at the head of the table. But he keeps his distance. "Baby girl," he greets me coolly, his gaze predatory and his deep voice edged with a husky, controlled joy.

"You won't be able to call me that in the meeting," I say, drawing closer to him, but not close enough to touch him. *That* would be dangerous.

"No," he drawls, and he's staring at my parted lips. "But I can call you that now."

His voice. So deep and graveled. Thick with husky intent. How will this work? How will we function like regular people when the allure is this manic? I try to distract myself. I pull my eyes away, forcing myself to calm down. I continue placing the papers around the table. "How'd it go with Max? Everything okay?"

"No. Not even close. He's coming in this afternoon so we can make a plan. The press is in on it now, which makes everything ten times more complicated. And a lot more expensive."

I'm not used to seeing him so on edge. Most of the time we've spent together, he's been relaxed. Okay, not entirely *relaxed*. But easy enough to soothe. The urge to comfort him now is too strong. I go to him, allowing myself one little indulgence...my fingers smooth an unruly strand of his hair into place. "Is there anything I can do?"

He opens his leather briefcase, as though to distract himself. "We'll have to go through all the particulars and sort through them. Throw down some hush money if necessary. I don't know why he can't keep it on the straight and narrow. My brother has a knack for pushing every boundary." Which I sort of already know.

I'm still touching the coarse silk of his hair. I skim my fingers along the line of his jaw, loving the textures of him. The smoothness of his recent shave underlaid by a barely-detectable roughness. The plump curve of his lower lip. My craving for him is pulsing in me, along with the beat of my heart.

He isn't breathing well. "Lexi. Why don't you sit in that chair. Or stand over there for a minute. It's probably not a good idea for you to touch me right now."

My hand stills, but I can't quite bring myself to draw away. "Why not?"

He pauses before giving me a gruff reply. "Because I get a fucking raging hard-on whenever you do. And as much as I enjoy raging hard-ons, they're not ideal in editorial meetings."

I wish he hadn't told me that. His anger only feeds my desire, inflaming it. I feel feverish. Alive. And so in love my heart aches.

And I can't do it.

I can't *not* give in to the most potent addiction I've ever known.

I glance at the clock on the wall. 8:29. Feigning obedience, I step away from him. Instead of sitting down, though, I walk over to the door and enter the code I've now memorized. The code to lock us in. There's a window to the hallway, a single pane of glass that runs the length of the door, but it's etched and opaque.

Rafe watches me walk back over to him, his eyes so dark they look almost black. I've gazed into them enough to know they're not black at all. They change with his moods, from a royal blue to the darkest indigo.

He's reading my intent. "Lexi—" He's watching my face, and his question gets lost in his breathing, in the intensity of his awareness of me as I stand close to him. Very close.

"It's only eight-thirty," I say. He's watching my mouth. He's flustered. And I'll admit it: I *love* flustering him. I crazy-love him when his big, musclebound body reacts to me in a way that's beyond his control. All that wide-shouldered, dark, masculine bravado. *Mine*. My basest urges are on overdrive. He's far too tempting. "They won't be here until nine."

He looks staggered. Ridiculously sexy. Torn, by a conflicted, ravenous need. Still, he protests. "Lexi," he says, his sternness underlaid with raw desire. "Be reasonable."

I stand on my toes, licking the lightest touch along his lower lip. "This *is* me being reasonable. What I *really* want to do would take much longer."

He stares down at me, incredulous.

But when I run my hand over the front of his pants, he's fully, ragingly hard. I kiss him again, licking my tongue between his lips. "I know how to make you come quickly. Let me."

"*Damn it*, Lexi," he growls, his breath quickening. I'm already unbuckling his belt and he makes no move to stop me. "*Fuck*."

"I want you," I whisper, kissing him again.

"Yes. You want me. You have me. And you're going to be the fucking undoing of me. Which you already know."

"I *am* going to undo you," I croon, owning his surrender. I know he won't refuse me. He can't. He's as needy for my touch as I am for his. "Like this." I unzip him, reaching into his pants and grasping my tight fist around the hot immensity of him. "The door is locked. No one can see us. No one knows what I'm about to do to you."

His eyes are narrowed, almost furious. Letting me do whatever I want. *Challenging* me to do whatever I want.

"I'm going take you into my mouth," I purr. "I'm going to suck on you and use both hands to –"

"*Lexi. Fuck–*"

"Do you want me to stop?"

"*No.*"

I squeeze him, working my hands along his length in careful, provocative strokes. I grip him harder, rubbing and teasing, totally focused on his pleasure.

Rafe groans.

"Look at you. You're already starting to come a little." It's true. I use the moisture to wet the head of his cock until he's slippery.

His expression is severe. A mixture of fury and ecstasy. He obeys me, watching my playful fingers.

"Be very quiet," I tell him. I pull a chair closer and sit down in front of him.

"Lexi," he breathes, as I lick my tongue over the gathering moisture, tasting him, nipping and kissing his silky hardness. His eyes close. "—*oh, God help me.*"

I lick again, gently sucking him deeper into my mouth as I hold him in my supple grip.

"*Oh, fuck.*" His groan is too loud.

"Quiet," I say.

Distant voices can be heard outside, out in the open area, but there's no one at the door. Yet. Rafe goes very still and I suck on him hungrily, easing him deeper, drawing on him with building, circular suction. With my hands and my mouth, I increase the pace. He exhales a curse and I can tell he's close. My fingers explore secret, intimate avenues, until his thick cum spills into my mouth in sudden, furtive bursts. I can't take all of it and it drips down my chin.

Okay, wow.

It takes him a minute to recover.

He grabs the small pile of napkins I'd put on the table next to my coffee cup. He uses them to wipe his cum from my face.

"*Jesus Christ*," he breathes, tipping my face up to him. He pulls me up and holds me close. "That was—"

"I love you," I whisper.

His color is high, his eyes volatile yet awed. He blinks, a slow, enchanted sweep that reminds me of moonlight over the water during our nights in Hawaii. He smooths a strand of my hair back into place. "You are so in for it tonight."

I tuck him back into his pants and help him fasten them. Then I step away from him. "I'll look forward to it, Mr. Black," I say, with business-like, assistant/junior partner-worthy subservience.

"So will I, Mrs. Black."

He stops me in my tracks with that one. *Mrs. Black.* Hearing him say it sends little darts of too many emotions to name through my soul.

"All right?" he says to me.

I nod.

Rafe goes to the door and enters the code and the door clicks open.

Just then, two men and a woman approach the door, talking, entering Rafe's office. They're followed by nine more people.

The meeting has begun.

6

———

RAFE

FUCK.

The team of executives walks into the room, talking and laughing like it's any other day. Like all this shit is normal. Like I'm not walking some fine line between heaven and hell. The heaven part begins to dissipate, speared by the sudden intrusion of twelve of my top employees.

And the hell is about to get a whole lot more intense.

I'm still trying to recalibrate after an impromptu orgasm that was so quick-rising and mind-blowing that I'm still reeling. I feel like my heart is beating somewhere outside my chest, exposed and bloody for everyone to see. I have to glance down for a second just to make sure I'm fucking zipped up.

Even worse, sitting right across the table from me is

Eric *fucking* Scully. A guy who's worked for me for three or four years, who's friendly enough, who I've socialized with from time to time and gotten to know.

Who was there that night.

Watching her.

What the fuck had I been thinking? How did I allow things to get that out of hand? I was completely unprepared for her reaction. Yeah, I'd revved her up. For *me*. So *I* could tease her and torture her like she's done to me since the minute she swanned into my life like a million-watt lightning bolt of sexuality whose sole intent was to twist my heart and my soul into roped, tightening pleasure-knots.

I hadn't predicted exactly *how* turned on those beads would get her. She came right there at the fucking poker table, like a goddess Greek mythology had forgotten to document. The Goddess of Jackpots and Orgasms.

And he was there, *watching her*. Now, the memory is almost too rage-inducing to handle. If I could block it out I would, but it flashes through my mind in excruciating play-by-play detail. Josh. Cole. Fucking Max.

And Eric Scully. He'd even said something, like he couldn't believe it. He'd been coveting her.

Mine.

He's watching her now. I can see it on his face: he's remembering how she looked. *The soft moans she made.*

I'm about to fucking lose it. My inner caveman is seriously considering breaking free.

But Lexi's looking at me. She can tell I'm about to go
ballistic, maybe. She's watching my expression, reading it.
She places her hand on my thigh, under the table. She just
leaves it there, holding me in place. She recognizes him, of
course she does. She knows what's going through my
mind.

It's good. That light warmth calms me a little, diffusing
a single degree of my fury.

I have to take it.

I have to own up to the fact that it was my own
goddamn fault. For putting her in that position. For not
letting her come before the start of the poker game, when
she'd asked for it. *Begged* for it. I've been blinded and
blind-sided by this tsunami of lust that's so new to me. Of
course I've experienced lust before, but not like this.
Nothing like this. This lust is madness-edged and brutal.
Like it has one hand gripped around my heart and the
other grasped tightly around my cock.

That old version of myself was entranced by Lexi
Blondeau. Turned on as fuck. Now, I'm so in love with her I can
barely see straight. The emotions are ten times more complex.
And if I'm going to spend a lifetime both protecting her while
simultaneously allowing her to exist and work and live her
life, I'm going to have to cowboy up and calm the fuck down.

Eric Scully isn't the only one riveted by Lexi. They're all staring at her. Her eyes match the sea-green of her dress. A few tendrils of her hair escaped the clip she pinned it up with, framing her face in elegant coils. Her lips are pink and almost-swollen...*from the blow job she just gave me.*

God help me.

Her right hand rests on my leg. And her left hand, gently clasped around a mug of coffee, displays the ring. One million dollars' worth of Tiffany's finest.

"Nice to see you all," I begin, willing my own steadiness. I don't want to fuck around. It's better to just get right to the heart of the fucking matter. And it turns out to be easier to do than I thought. I *am* steady when it comes to work and leadership within the company I've built from the ground up. As long as I focus on them—and not on *her*—I'm fine. My voice sounds unwavering, almost arrogant. Which is also fine. Better to come across as a prick than a pussy-whipped mess. "Most of you know by now that I've hired a new assistant. This is Lexi Blondeau."

Lexi smiles, shyly but with an edge. She's changed over the past few weeks. She always exuded a kind of sensual prowess, even if she wasn't aware of it. She'd bowled me over with it the first moment I laid eyes on her. Now, she's more experienced. She knows her own influence. It sort of radiates from her along with her golden glow.

"As some of you might have heard," I continue, "Lexi is

now not only my new assistant, she's also my fiancée. We plan to marry soon."

I let this information settle for a few seconds. There are some surprised murmurs. A few of them offer their congratulations. Olivia Beckett, executive editor of the Fashion section of the lifestyle magazine, obviously hasn't heard the news. Her eyes widen. I'd been encouraged to head-hunt her from another magazine about two years ago. I offered her big money to jump ship and she's worked out well. The fashion shoots receive glowing reviews and have been called "hip, must-have and oh so L.A." by the Los Angeles Times, a quote that's become a sort of tag line for the department. Olivia's staring at the ring. And I happen to know the first fucking person she'll call with the news.

Vanessa.

I let the unpleasantness of *that* realization drift. I haven't thought much about my ex since Lexi showed up on the scene. I've mostly ignored Vanessa's irate phone calls. To be honest, I'm fully aware I've been a complete asshole to her. I'm not proud of it, but in my mind, the whole thing was well and truly over before Lexi's job interview ever even happened. I'd made that very clear. At least I thought I had. The problem was, Vanessa is a high maintenance bitch of the highest order who was never going to give up without a fight.

The entire scenario is irritating me. When I speak

again, I sound pissed off. Which is probably a good thing. I don't want any misunderstandings about the next detail. "Lexi just graduated from Stanford. She has some business and publishing experience and will be working alongside me, closely, and in whatever capacity I choose. With my assistance—and yours—she'll be learning the ropes. The ins and outs of the entire company. She'll spend time in each department, to be informed directly by each of you. I want her to learn the workings of Downtown from the ground up. So I'll thank you in advance for welcoming her and guiding her in whatever way she requires as she settles into her new role."

I glare at Eric Scully. *Except yours*, is what I'm thinking. Cole and Josh are young. Max is a different story altogether. But I have the distinct urge to fire Eric's smug ass right here on the spot. I know he thinks of himself as a ladies' man. I know he works out every day at lunchtime. I know he's competitive as fuck, which is part of the reason I hired him in the first place. At this exact moment, that detail is pissing me off.

I don't react. And I inwardly applaud myself on my restraint. I can sack him later if the need arises. If he makes one wrong move, he's history. Until then, I have enough on my plate besides looking around for a new senior executive editor. The guy has around twelve degrees and is therefore probably smart enough to figure out that I'll happily throttle him if he so much as touches a hair on her pretty little head.

He sees the look I give him. He says something polite and non-suggestive to Lexi and she smiles briefly as her cheeks go pink—*keep calm, Rafe*—as she acknowledges him, before turning to the next person as I begin to introduce them, one by one.

Then it's on to the next item on the agenda, which is them filling me in on all I've missed since I've been away. Taking my spur-of-the-moment hiatus from life so I could gorge myself on her beauty and her sweetness. Her smile and her laughter. Her initiation and her satiation. *Her luscious body and that tight little—*

No.

Do. Not. Think. About. Her.

Fuck.

It's agonizing, with her hand still resting on my thigh like that.

I stare at Olivia Beckett, who's speaking. I concentrate on her bulky glasses and her beaky face. The way her hair is scraped back. She's working some odd look that might be edgily fashionable—I wouldn't have a clue—but it's doing her no favors. I wonder, and not for the first time, what she and Vanessa ever had in common. My ex-girlfriend is a successful model who Olivia recruited to write a monthly column for the magazine about a year ago, which is how we met. A day in the life of a jet-setting supermodel, that kind of thing. It had been Olivia's idea.

Listening to Olivia's boring monotone as she talks about her vision for the next fashion spread is helping. My hard-on is back under control.

Which is a very good thing, because my phone rings and it's a call I'll need to take. A police detective. Max mentioned him this morning. He wants to speak to me about the accusation against Max for insider trading that my brother is tangled up in. I've already made up my mind to do everything I can to pay our way out of it, if it comes to that. I know I might have to spend the next few hours dealing with whatever it is this cop is going to tell me.

I stand up. "Sorry, I have to take this."

I make a decision, even though I know it'll have a major downside: *that* downside, though, is a million times more palatable than picturing Eric Scully drooling all over Lexi for the rest of the day. I need to know where she'll be. Who she'll be with.

I need to concentrate.

"Olivia," I say. "Show Lexi around today. Give her a tour of the Fashion department and introduce her to your people. Looks like I could be tied up for a while." I realize how fucking abrupt I sound. "Thank you," I add. I'm usually a little more dedicated to my people skills but today is already having its way with me. I've been given a practically-public blow job by my unbelievably hot nymph of a fiancée and my brother is about to get arrested.

I glance at Lexi. "You all right?"

"Fine." She smiles. "I'll see you later."

I have an urge to tell her I love her, but I'm aware of the twelve other pairs of eyes staring at me. Certain revelations will undoubtedly cross her path today that might shake her. I wish now that I'd prepared her for what she's about to learn. I hadn't wanted to spoil any of the moments we've so far shared with sordid details about my bitch of an ex. But I wish to hell right now that I'd done it anyway.

It's one of the most difficult things I've ever done in my life. Leaving her there. Pathetic, possibly. I don't even fucking care. I feel like scooping her up and taking her away with me, to someplace where we can be alone and talk and laugh and make love in that insanely beautiful way we have. *So I can wrap myself around her. So I can kiss her and touch her. So I can get inside, where I belong.*

It's all I really want to do.

Instead, I open the door and close it behind me as I answer the phone. "Rafe Black."

"Mr. Black, this is Detective Frank Malone with the LAPD. How are you this morning?"

"Fine. You?"

"I've been better. Despite my track record, I don't enjoy putting people away. I'm going cut right to the chase: the SEC is demanding justice. Someone's head has to roll, Mr.

Black. Your brother's laptop was seized and we have enough evidence to put him away for ten years."

Ten years? Fucking hell. "I'm sure we can come to an agreement, Detective. I have very deep pockets."

"They're not going to be satisfied with a pay-off with this particular case, Mr. Black. They want blood and they want time. I suggest you meet with your brother, prep your lawyers to within an inch of their lives, and get ready to write some fat checks. Even so, you'll be lucky if he gets less than two years."

I run a hand through my hair. My skin feels clammy as a low-strung terror ices through my veins. Max spent over a year in juvie from the age of eleven years old. He came out a changed kid, which isn't surprising. He looks tough but his chasms of vulnerability are somehow still one of the most pronounced things about him. My heart skips a couple of beats at the thought of Max behind bars, again. My little punk of a brother who's had every hard knock life could cough up. Because of that, he can never quite shake his fuck you attitude.

I suppress the urge to swear at and/or threaten Detective Malone. "I'll be in touch as soon as we've met with our lawyers, Detective."

"Make it sooner rather than later. An arrest will be issued next Friday if we haven't heard from you by then."

The line goes dead.

I lean against the wall for a second, feeling suddenly

drained. I wish I could take him away, too, and hide him somewhere. Hawaii. Paris. Brazil. Anywhere. He could simply disappear, change his identity, live out his life in a beachfront condo in Rio or somewhere. If I thought it would work, I'd suggest it. But Max doesn't follow rules. He wouldn't stay put or abide by an imposed lock-down. He'd turn up in New York or L.A., or get pinged by some power-happy border control officer once the heat died down. It would never work.

I call my lawyers.

OLIVIA BECKETT LEADS me through the maze of offices toward the Fashion department. We walk past the door of the senior executive editor's office. *Eric Scully.* Of course I recognized him at the meeting, but I didn't want to escalate the situation. Rafe was barely able to sit there without lunging across the table. Anyway, the night of the poker game was, to be honest, a total blur. I'd hardly noticed those other men. I only noticed *him.*

"Rafe said you have some experience in business, and in publishing. Do you have any experience in fashion?" Olivia asks me. She says his name like they know each other well. Is it because she's one of his executives? Or some other reason? I'm reminded that there's so much about Rafe I still don't know.

"No," I admit. I'm hardly going to tell her the real

reasons I never took much of an interest in fashion. It's not the kind of information you can breezily chitchat about. *Actually, I grew up destitute. For most of my childhood I was lucky to get a new outfit a year. I wore my clothes until they became threadbare. I learned to sew so I could stitch a length of old denim to my jeans so the kids at school wouldn't laugh at how short my pants were. I used the one wool blanket on my bed to sew patches onto the elbows of my sweater. And then, once I could afford better clothes with the miniscule amount of money I earned from my part-time jobs, I wore baggy, unfashionable outfits intentionally. I know, right? And a pair of ugly glasses I bought in a thrift shop for three dollars, which I only ditched a couple of weeks ago. Why? Because I wanted to be invisible. Because I didn't want men chasing after me the way he used to threaten to do. And others who came later, once I was passed from one foster family to the next.*

I don't, of course, mention any of that. "I've spent most of my time over the past few years studying. But my best friend is a fashion blogger. She's taught me a few things. Or at least she's trying."

I'm attempting to make small talk, but Olivia eyes me, straight-faced, taking in my outfit. I'm getting the vibe that she thinks I've somehow encroached on territory that, in her mind, belongs to someone else. *Who*, I'm not sure.

I realize I've changed. I don't feel intimidated by Olivia Beckett in the slightest. Two weeks ago, I probably would have wilted under her judgmental scrutiny. Rafe has changed me, yes, but *my* effect on *him* has changed me just as much his effect on me has. The fact is, I have no doubt he'd fire her at the drop of a hat if I asked him to.

Luckily, I'm not that petty.

Or that thin-skinned. I've dealt with things much worse than Olivia Beckett's disapproval, or whatever this is.

I'm distracted and a little agog at the scene as we walk through the Fashion department. There are expansive views of the pool and the city in every direction. Models and mannequins are being fitted by teams of busy, flamboyant designers who pin and primp the outfits with dramatic, fussy dedication. Olivia leads me into her corner office. Her gigantic white desk is covered in artfully-strewn photographs and magazines. Next to the desk are several racks laden with colorful, cutting-edge garments.

"You know," she says, "I was a little surprised by the news of Rafe's engagement to you, if you don't mind me saying. We all thought he was on the verge of proposing to someone else."

A cool wash of...something, races through my veins. Rafe never mentioned a past girlfriend. The only thing he said was that he'd never taken anyone besides Max to his house in Hawaii. That was the only conversation we had about his "other women." I never doubted Rafe *had* other women in his life, before me. Looking like he does and just being like he…is. Even with this new information, though, I don't doubt him. If there had been someone else in his life that day of my job interview, I have a feeling it would have been over from the moment he poured me that very first glass of champagne. Even so, I take Olivia's bait. "Really? Who?"

"They'd been dating for quite a while. Six or seven months, off and on. Well, mainly *on*. I'm pretty sure it was exclusive. At least it was on *her* part. She's a good friend of mine and she's been in a total state about it. Heartbroken, basically. She really thought it was the real thing. He called her a few weeks ago and suddenly, just out of the blue, broke it off. Rafe hasn't been answering any of her calls." Why is she telling me all this? "I mean, I wouldn't even mention it to you, except that it was just so unexpected when he announced your engagement. He's talked to her a couple of times since he called it off, but he won't agree to see her. I guess he's been busy."

Yes, I guess you could say that.

Rafe had occasionally turned on his phone in Hawaii to check on how things were going with Max. Every time, it immediately started ringing off the hook. Calls he ignored. At the time I thought it work-related stuff.

Apparently not. "He never mentioned any of that to me."

"Really?" says Olivia. "That's so strange. I wonder why

he wouldn't." Is she trying to rile me? To make me doubt him? I *am* riled, but not in the way she might think. Rafe was trying to protect me. He didn't tell me because he didn't want other people and their dramas to intrude on our secluded, magical time together. At least that's what I want to believe. Why is it that when Rafe and I are together, nothing else matters and the world feels like it has been sprinkled with fairy dust, but the minute we're apart, everything gets thorny and complicated? "She's due to come in today. We have a meeting about her column."

"Oh."

"In about half an hour, actually. We're doing a tie-in with the photo shoot she's in, for the December issue."

"She's a model?" This doesn't shock me, for some reason.

"One of the highest paid models in the world, as a matter of fact, for the past two years in a row. I'm sure you've heard of her. Vanessa Beale."

Vanessa Beale. Of course I've heard of her. Her face is everywhere. It seems amazing, suddenly, that I don't already know this. Rafe is L.A. royalty, according to Tess. And Vanessa Beale is...Vanessa Beale. Then again, I haven't done a lot of googling lately. And there was that whole thing about Rafe's virtual footprint being erased every three minutes.

"Rafe doesn't know Vanessa's due in today," Olivia

informs me. "Otherwise I'm pretty sure he wouldn't have assigned me to be your chaperone today." She's amused.

My chaperone. The word implies that she's babysitting the boss's over-indulged flavor-of-the-month for an hour or two. Olivia Beckett is really starting to rub me the wrong way. Then again, at least she's given me a heads-up, that I'm about to come face to face with Rafe's possibly-psycho ex.

"I would have filled Rafe in on the schedule," Olivia says, "but I know he has a lot on his plate right now. What with Max's...issues." Her smile mellows into one that could almost be genuine. "I'm sure we can handle it, though, right, Lexi? I mean, you've got the ring—and *wow*, is all I can say—so there's hardly anything to worry about. Vanessa will get over it. Eventually. I've already told her to move on. Plenty more fish in the sea and all that."

I think we both know there aren't many fish in the sea like Rafe Black.

Was he dating Vanessa when he met me? Had he dumped her *before* I stepped into his life...or after? Does it matter?

Someone walks in.

She's early, what do you know.

I recognize her immediately. From a thousand photographs.

Vanessa Beale stands there looking like she just stepped off the cover of Vogue. Which she probably has.

Her long, dark hair gleams. Her slim, practically-emaciated body showcases her white couture jumpsuit in a way only a fashion model could pull off. Her pale skin is flawless, her red lips bee-stung. And her eyes, rimmed with kohl and spidery eyelashes, fix themselves onto me with feral intensity. "Is this her?" she asks Olivia, as though I might be a mannequin who can't hear or speak. I never expected Rafe not to have a past. I guess I didn't expect his past to be so...present. But I can't quite summon the jealousy, or even the rivalry. The searing intimacy of my time with Rafe is too close to me and too reassuring.

"Lexi Blondeau, meet Vanessa Beale."

"I wish I could say it was a pleasure," says Vanessa coldly. Her black eyes dart to the ring on my finger, which causes a slight pinkening of her cheeks.

It's one of my weaknesses: I can't help sympathizing. I'm used to being looked down on, after all my years of hiding behind frumpy clothes and junk shop glasses. I know what it feels like to live your life at the bottom of the heap. Now that I've ditched the heap altogether and am now living somewhere up among the stars, it's hard to get my bearings. The shift is still so new, and my first instinct is to try to ease the tension.

"Nice to meet you, Vanessa," I say, even though this whole thing is wildly awkward. "Olivia was just telling me about your amazing career."

Vanessa eyes me, not expecting friendliness. I can see

her confusion flickering: *Is she serious, dumb, or just being a total bitch?* She can't quite tell.

So I keep talking. "Your column sounds so interesting."

"How...*old* are you?" she blurts out, glaring at my face.

I almost lie. But my age shouldn't feel like some crime Rafe has committed. I don't have anything to hide from Vanessa Beale. "Twenty. Why?"

Vanessa laughs, but there's no humor in it. "Of course you are."

I'm not sure how to respond to this, so I don't.

"How did you and Rafe meet?" she says. "I'm dying to know."

"I applied for a job. As his assistant."

She laughs again. "Don't tell me. You got the job."

"Um...yes." Sort of. *The details of my appointment have changed slightly, though, since he first offered it. Quite drastically, in fact. From assistant to business partner. Plus I get to fuck him whenever I feel like it. Just this morning—you won't believe this—I sucked him off right there in his office. God, he was so damn big and bossy and so totally* mine. *He came so unbelievably hard.*

Down girl.

Vanessa looks unsettled.

"I'm sorry about the way it's turned out between you and Rafe." I probably shouldn't have said that, even if it was a genuine attempt to be kind.

And I can't really feel bad or guilty about being swept away by the man I'm about to marry.

Olivia closes the door of her office, and this feels ominous. Like things are about to happen that she wants to keep out of public view. Vanessa's face has turned a darker shade of pink, creeping up her neck like a stain. "You man-stealing bitch!" she screams, actually stamping one of her feet.

Am I? It's true that only one thing crossed my mind when I meet Rafe: *I want him.* More than I'd wanted safety or guarantees. Now, my feelings are a thousand times more intense. Rafe is my haven. He's the one and only person I've ever known in this stormy, daunting, lonely life who's made me feel wanted. And like I'm not just surviving but fully *alive.* In some weird way, I feel like Rafe introduced me to myself. To the me that's allowed to breathe and thrive and feel, without fear. Without that stomach-curling panic that lodged itself into my soul at a very early age and never, ever let go. Rafe unraveled that fear. He's starting to actually *fix* it. With his lust and his love and his protective-ness. I love him more than I've ever loved anyone or anything.

And I'm not about to give him up.

Apparently Vanessa doesn't want to give Rafe up either. Her fury takes me a little off-guard. "You seduced him! You fucking *stole* him! He was supposed to propose to *me.* He was *going* to, before you came along and fucked everything up! You're a gold-digging *whore*, that's what you are!"

Wow.

"Vanessa," Olivia says. "I think we all just need to calm down a little."

"You're just after him for his *money!*" Vanessa screeches. "I *know* your type. You have no money or talent or career of your own, so you attach yourself onto some super-rich sugar daddy and bleed him dry. I know exactly what you're doing. You won't get away with this!"

I'll admit it, the accusation stings a little. Some tiny corner of my soul flinches.

"You reeled him in with your face and that...*that body. Blinding* him to who you really are by offering him on-call sex. Admit it! What else do you have to offer him? *Nothing,* that's what. Nothing!"

What *do* I have to offer Rafe? Besides love and devotion and...amazingly hot sex? Is that enough?

"Vanessa–" Olivia tries again.

"Oh, don't worry," Vanessa shrieks. "I'm done with her. But I'm not done with *him*. There's no way I'm fucking done with him! I'm going to tell him *everything*. I'm going to expose you for what you are, you little man-stealing bitch!"

Despite everything, it hurts. I force myself not to react. I know I shouldn't let her affect me like this.

"I love him!" Vanessa's crying now. "And he loves me!

He *told* me that. He said those words to me. And you *stole* him! Did he tell you that he talked to me while he was in Hawaii? What does that say about how he really feels? Did he tell you we'd talked about a ring? And where we'd honeymoon? Paris, he said. Did he tell you *that*? Do you even care about *him*, or just his money? Once I explain things to him...once he sees you for what you really are, he'll change his mind about you, you'll see. He'll come back to me and we'll be together. Like we're meant to be."

Vanessa bursts into tears and Olivia pats her arm and hands her some tissues.

Vanessa blows her nose in a loud, un-supermodelish honk.

"I think I should go." I wish I could say the thought of Vanessa ranting all this to Rafe doesn't bother me. Of course it won't change anything. Of course he won't listen.

Or will he?

He told her they'd honeymoon in Paris? That's exactly what he'd said to me.

"No." Vanessa pulls herself together, checking her now-blotchy face in a silver compact she pulls from her designer handbag. "*I'm* going. Olivia, I'll call you later about the column. But first, there's someone I need to see."

That would be Rafe, I'm guessing.

Will he agree to see her? Will it matter? *Will I find myself back on the streets, alone, where I belong, possibly? Maybe she's right.*

Vanessa strides toward the door. Before opening it, she turns and hisses, "You might have sunk your claws into him with your skanky bimbo trailer trash charms, but he'll tire of meaningless sex soon enough. He'll beg to have me back because we're alike. We're on the same wavelength and we're similar people. You'll see."

She slams the door behind her, causing a few papers to fall from Olivia's desk.

Holy shit.

I exhale slowly, wishing things could be easy, for once. But they never are. Except when Rafe and I are together, shut away from the world and all its manic demands for strength.

Olivia is surprisingly sympathetic. "Honey, she's a supermodel. It's all drama with them. I said it before and I'll say it again: you've got the ring. Believe you me, she worked it with everything she had, but in the end she never quite managed to get that bling on her finger. Rafe Black doesn't hand out a Tiffany rock like that one without wanting it right where it is. Plenty of girls have tried, trust me on that."

I suddenly feel exhausted. I can admit my first impression of Olivia Beckett wasn't entirely positive, but now I can see she'd only been gearing up for the melodrama she clearly knew was coming. Now, she seems to understand that my emotions have been shaken to the core. She picks up her phone. "Darla, we need two skim double-shot lattes and four Godiva dark chocolates. And bring me the specs for the desert hobo shoot."

She ends the call and motions for me to sit. "Rule number one at Downtown. When you're at work you're at work. We're type-A geniuses with big balls and thick skins, or we wouldn't be here. You must have some of that in you, girl, or you wouldn't have gotten that job interview in the first place. You went to Stanford and you've landed Rafe Black. Pick yourself up and dust yourself off and let's get on with the rest of our day."

Since that's pretty much exactly what I've been doing my entire life, I switch gears into my keep-going-no-matter-what default. For the next seven solid hours, I put all my emotional baggage aside, make all attempts *not* to think about Vanessa confronting Rafe with her tirade. Or how he might react to it. Or whether or not this will change anything between us.

Olivia strides around and multi-tasks manically for the rest of the day, until I feel like I've been mentored to within in an inch of my life. I meet photographers, editors-at-large, designers, models, seamstresses and fashion types of every description. Many have no idea I'm Rafe's fiancée, or even care, which is just fine with me.

In those passing moments when I'm able to put Vanessa's wrath, Max's black cloud and even Rafe's...*omission* out of my mind, the work day is everything I once dreamed about: challenging and engaging and fabulous. And when the echoes of Vanessa's harsh accusations creep in, my resolve and my love and my own indignation about everything I learned burns in me like a fever. I refuse to let her come between us or to change Rafe's mind. There's no way in hell I'm going to let that crazy bitch take away the most beautiful thing in my life.

No way.

But he sure does have a few things to explain.

8

———

RAFE

MY BROTHER IS SITTING in my office. As per his usual I-don't-give-a-fuck-about-anything attitude, he chose to wear his worn biker jacket—over a shirt and tie, at least—to the meeting with the lawyers. The top two buttons of his shirt are undone and his tie has been loosened, reminding me eerily of a noose. His tattoos are visible on his neck and he looks like he's been working out a lot. We're alone, after a grueling six-hour session with our legal team that cemented the fact that Max will probably do time. The best the lawyers are hoping for is that the authorities will agree to a pay-out and/or—depending on the judge—Max will get sentenced one-year in a minimum security prison, with the possibility of parole after three months. They're going to give it everything they have. Which happens to be a shitload of my money, but whatever. He might be put away as soon as next week.

Max knows where I keep my Scotch and helps himself to a generous helping, tipping it back before recharging his glass and pouring me one.

My phone vibrates again and I check to see who it is. I haven't heard from Lexi all day and I miss her so much my chest literally aches. But it's not Lexi. It's Vanessa. Again. Odds are she's definitely heard the news about my engagement.

Only Max and his impending incarceration could keep me away from Lexi for this long. I know he needs me right now. The shadows under his eyes have that bruised look—along with the actual bruises from our punch-up, which I now almost regret—that means he hasn't been sleeping.

"It was a stupid fucking thing to do," I tell him. There's an email trail to prove that he traded insider information to the tune of five million dollars, which investigators found after seizing his laptop.

"No shit, professor. Thanks for the tip."

"*I* could've given you five million dollars, if you wanted it that badly. Instead I get to hand my money over to a rabid pack of lawyers and you get a ten-by-ten cell." Square footage will probably be the very least of Max's problems if he ends up inside.

"Next time I'll ask you first."

His complete lack of remorse pisses me off, but it's nothing new. Lecturing him, I know from experience, doesn't help.

"So," he says, changing the subject. "She said yes, huh?"

I watch him take another swig of his drink, wishing there was more I could have done to shield him. His hair is disheveled and he looks exhausted. If I could rewind time, I would. I'd somehow figure out how to pre-empt the bad shit that happened to him all those years ago. "Yeah, she did."

"You lucky bastard."

"I only hope I can be good enough for her." It sounds cheesy, but it's true.

"Trust me, you can't." Max exhales a laugh and tips back the rest of his drink. "Seriously, though, congratulations. When's the big day?"

"We want to do it soon." If we want Max to be there, we might have to have the wedding as soon as this weekend. I pause before saying it. "Thanks for calling me the other night, by the way."

He's quiet for a couple of seconds. "Of course I was going to call you, Rafe."

The silence is connective. Despite the fuck-ups, and under all that tough-guy exterior, my brother is still the best person I know.

"How did you propose?"

"At home. On my knees with a million dollar ring, hoping like hell she'd say yes."

Max smiles. "Shit." There are only two people on the planet that have the ability to make me feel like I'm not made of the stone I usually force myself to be. And, strangely, knowing that my brother shares a connection with Lexi makes me love her even more, just because, on some level, he does too.

"If it's too soon for her," I say, "we'll wait. Until you can be there."

"Don't wait, just on my account," Max says. "I wouldn't want you to do that. You two go ahead and get started with your life together. Don't let me hold you up."

It doesn't seem fair, that even all the money in the world can't save my brother. He just about breaks my jaded heart sometimes. "Well, that's too fucking bad. Because I'm not getting married without a best man. If I get my way, we'll do it this Saturday."

Max pauses, and for a second he reminds me so much of his ten-year-old self I almost go to him, to give him a goddamn hug or something. Sick regret churns in my stomach, at an old memory that still has the capacity to cut me like a knife. My brother can read the turn of my thoughts, and he quickly changes the subject. "So, what about that other chick you were dating? The supermodel?"

"That was already over. But Olivia Beckett was showing Lexi around today. There's no doubt Olivia was on her phone to Vanessa as soon as I left the room this morning."

Max laughs. "Why didn't you get someone else to show Lexi around?"

"Because if it wasn't her, I had a feeling it would have somehow ended up being Eric Scully."

He grins at me. "Ah."

"Yeah."

"Never thought I'd see the day my brother would morph into the jealous type. That must mean it's the real thing."

"It sure feels like the real thing," I tell him. "The realest fucking thing that's ever happened to me."

"It's pretty obvious she feels the same way, Rafe." After a pause, Max says, "I'm sorry about this whole insider trading fiasco." Max's rebellious streak is so ingrained he doesn't even realize he's doing it half the time. But even with the emails, something about the whole thing doesn't quite add up. I'm not entirely sure he's guilty. Even if he is, there's something about him you just can't stay mad at.

"Anyway," I say, "you hungry? Lexi's friend Tess is coming to our place for dinner tonight. You should come. Filet mignon and a nice Bordeaux."

Max smiles, maybe at the way I'm already calling my apartment "our" place. "Sure. We can celebrate your engagement."

When we get back to the apartment, Lexi and Tess are already there, sitting in the hot tub outside. Despite Tess and Max, seeing Lexi after almost eight hours—*in her bikini*—all wet and hot and more stunningly gorgeous than I can handle, I can't help myself. I have to kiss her. Not just kiss her but *kiss* her. I touch my tongue to her lips, easing into her mouth. She tries to pull back but I hold my hand against her hair, to keep her there. I'm dizzy from the taste of her. I'm slayed by her beauty. I'm besotted and lust-drunk. I can't see straight.

"Don't mind him," I vaguely hear Max say to Tess. "He finally met his match."

Lexi breaks the kiss and looks up at me. I'm expecting it: the questions behind her eyes—which are an even brighter green than I remember from this morning. Clearly, she's heard about the psycho-drama involving my ex. She might have even witnessed some of it first-hand. I've got some explaining to do, which I'll do as soon as we're alone. "I missed you," I tell her. "How was your day?"

She doesn't answer and is distracted by the fact that her friend is staring at Max like he's a piece of meat. Women tend to do that. "Tess," says Lexi. "You've met Rafe, and this is Rafe's brother Max."

Max goes through the pleasantries but this girl probably isn't his type. Not that Max really has a "type." He pretty much sleeps with any woman who happens to flick him a loaded glance. Or at least he used to. I haven't actually seen him with anyone in a while.

We have dinner. We talk a little about the engagement, but I don't bring up the wedding date. Tess mainly monopolizes Lexi's attention throughout, chattering on about her blog and some guy she met at a party, so after dinner Max and I go out onto the patio and smoke Cuban cigars as daylight fades.

"I think I'll head home," Max says, as soon as Tess has gushingly hugged everyone—including Max—and Lexi walks her to the door. Lexi's friend is definitely...enthusiastic. I guess it's been a while since she and Lexi spent time together.

Max makes a plan to see me tomorrow.

"Don't worry about anything," I tell him. "Chances are we'll still be able to buy you out of a prison sentence."

"Sure, Rafe. See you tomorrow." Like he couldn't care less one way or the other. When he kisses Lexi goodnight, on the cheek, I don't even mind. Her presence is helping him, I can see that, feeding something in his soul from afar.

And then it's just us.

Lexi doesn't say anything. She walks away, heading into my bedroom.

Okay, so she's peeved about whatever revelations came to light today.

I follow her.

The room is dimly lit but her hair catches light, as it always seems to do. She goes to the couch in the far corner of the room. She sits, curling her bare legs beneath her. She's wearing a short flowery pink dress over her bikini.

There's nothing overly provocative about the cut of the dress itself, but the shape she gives it somehow *makes* it provocative. I want to peel it off her, to feed my addiction, which is raging in me after our day apart. But I don't. I wait. I walk over and sit next to her on the couch, but not too close because she's watching me with an edge of that petulance that means she's mad at me.

I love that I can read this. That I'm learning the nuances of who she is. And I notice she's still wearing her ring, even if it's twisted around to hide the diamond. Whatever she thinks I've done, it's not bad enough to convince her to take off her ring.

Her sea-green eyes meet mine. She looks impossibly young and this detail reminds me of her past. Of those cold nights when she had to run and hide. Of how scared she must have been.

I don't care about mad. Mad I can handle. Breakable is what I'm worried about.

I watch her face for a few seconds. "I'm going to tell you everything you want to know, Lexi. I'll explain and you can ask me any questions you have, but I'll just start by saying this: I never loved her. I love *you*. Only you. You're the only woman I've ever loved." The words come out rasped because they're achingly true.

She listens, but she has some grievances she wants to talk through before she even thinks about forgiving me. "She came in to see Olivia this morning. We met."

Shit. "I'm...sure that didn't go very well. I'm sorry I didn't warn you."

"Why didn't you tell me about her?"

"Because she was already out of the picture. It was irrelevant."

"*She* didn't seem to think she was out of the picture. She still thinks she's very much *in* the picture."

"Well, she's wrong. I told her it was over. She ignored me, even though I was as clear as I could have been about it. I told her I didn't want to see her again." This whole argument is annoyingly petty. It's a woman thing, where you have to discuss every detail to death. Usually, I'd be irritated by this. But this is Lexi, of course, who skews everything. I won't just indulge her in whatever way she needs me to, I'll fucking get down on my knees and beg if I have to.

"Did she come see you today?" she asks.

"No, I've been at our lawyers' offices. If you'd like to check my phone you'll see that I have around twenty unanswered calls from her. But not one from the person I actually wanted to hear from."

She ignores this. "She said you were planning to propose to her. Is that true?"

Goddamn it. "Lexi. No. In *her* mind, maybe. But that was never going to happen. I don't propose to people I'm not head over heels in love with."

Nothing. She's not relenting. "She said you promised to

take her to Paris for the honeymoon." This detail pisses her off, maybe more than any other, I can tell by the way she says it. Still, I can't help but smile a little. It's ridiculous, that she's worried about any of this.

"And you *believed* that? Yes, I tell *all* the women I'm about to propose to that I'm going to take them to Paris. Just like I told you."

I can't tell if she's reading my sarcasm. She's glaring at me. "I guess I don't find all this as funny as you do."

I get down on my knees in front of her. I take her hand and she—just—allows this. "I don't find it funny, sweetheart. I find it unbelievable that you'd be bothered by any of it. Vanessa knows I own a small five-star hotel with a Michelin-rated restaurant on the left bank. She wanted me to take her there. She came up with big plans about it, which I didn't listen to because I already knew it was over between us. Which I told her. She ignored me and cried about it and basically stalked me even though I told her repeatedly that it was never going to happen between us."

Lexi's still watching me. I take my phone out of my pocket and bring up the recent calls. Then I start deleting all the ones that are from Vanessa. "I haven't explicitly said the words 'fuck off' because I was trying to be gentlemanly about it. I have no desire to ever see her again. What I had with Vanessa was never remotely satisfying to me. I never felt even a milli-second of real happiness when we were together. We argued a lot because she was constantly accusing me of being cold-hearted and distant and disinterested, which she was right about. I never loved her. I didn't even *like* her. I don't know why I agreed to date her in the first place."

"Maybe because she's so beautiful," Lexi says.

Another smile escapes me before I can stop it. Because her expression makes me...happy.

She's *jealous*.

God, I'm so in love with her. "Your jealousy might be the most adorable thing I've ever seen and also the greatest triumph of my entire life, but it's not necessary, Lex. I didn't find her beautiful at all. Her inner ugliness was always too close to the surface." I ease Lexi's ring around her finger so the diamond is resting on top. She seems to wear it this way, with the diamond inside her fist, like she's embarrassed or shy about our engagement. Like she doesn't want people to know. "*You*, on the other hand, blow my mind in every possible way. To call you beautiful doesn't do you justice. You're exquisite. Inside and out. You enchant me. I couldn't have *dreamed* you up. *I love you.* I want to *marry* you—right now, if you'll let me. Or on Saturday, on the beach in Malibu. And then I want to spend every day for the rest of my life with you, making you happy, taking you everywhere you want to go, taking care of you, giving you everything I have. Any other questions?"

She's starting to relent, but we're not quite there yet. "She called me a gold-digging whore."

I stare at her. *Fuck.* I run my fingers through my hair. What I really feel like doing is punching a wall. "Yeah, that sounds like something Vanessa would say. She used to call me a cocky bastard, a twisted, commitment-phobic jerk and a cold-hearted asshole, pretty much on a daily basis."

And there it is, the smallest hint of understanding in the torch-like glow in her eyes. "She did?"

"All the time."

"I'm also a man-stealing bitch."

"Well, I'm an arrogant prick."

She almost smiles. "That one's a little bit true."

Thank you, universe. She's almost making a joke. "I'm sorry you had to deal with all that, honey." I smile, almost beseechingly, and lace my fingers through hers. "I've got a thing for man-stealing bitches, just saying."

I search in her eyes for our connection, and find the guarded fringe of it. "I might have a small thing for arrogant pricks."

I feel like singing from the fucking rooftops. I'm starting to break through this wall between us, finally. "I'm sorry I didn't warn you about her. I should have. I didn't want to bring it up when we were in Hawaii. There didn't seem to be any point. Then I planned to show you around myself today, but with all of Max's shit going on, I got distracted. I should have been there for you, and I wasn't."

"You were helping Max. It's okay, Rafe. I didn't expect you to hold my hand all day. I just…I wasn't expecting it. I thought she might go to you and…"

"What, and change my mind about you? That would never happen, Lexi. It's impossible. You can't doubt me *that* easily, surely. Haven't I proven enough that I adore you? Tell me how I can convince you."

I'm still on my knees. Her toenails are painted pink. I even know what fucking shade of pink it is because I painted them when we were still in Hawaii: Cotton Candy. She'd been in a much better mood that day.

The toes. The long, tan legs. The pout. But she still hasn't forgiven me. "You told her you loved her. You talked to her when we were in Hawaii."

Usually, when a woman gets mad at me—and they always do—I feel almost relieved. *Finally, an out. I can get the fuck out of here. She wants to be left alone to stew in the quagmire of my misdemeanors. I can go home and have a drink and watch a baseball game until I fall asleep, alone. Without anyone criticizing or bitching or inflicting their pettiness onto my life.*

Now, all I want to do is prove myself to her and roll around in the forgiveness I'll beg for if I have to. I decide to start with being honest.

I sit on the couch next to her, still holding her hand. I lean back into the seat and I start talking. "I met her in a meeting that had to do with her column, when it was first starting up. After the meeting, she asked for my phone number. I didn't give it to her, but I saw her again a few months later and she asked again. I had an extra ticket to a charity dinner so I thought, what the hell, I'll take her. I hadn't been on a date for a while and I thought maybe it would be good for me to get out for a change and do something other than work late and fall asleep at my desk."

Lexi's listening, watching my face, letting me play lightly with her fingers, so I keep going.

"So we went on this date and she was so *into* it and somehow one date turned into two. It was before I knew how bitchy and calculating she was. She was still acting like a semi-normal person in those early days, hiding the sides of her personality that I would later learn are the *main* parts of her personality. The pettiness and that sense that she was always being wronged by everyone around her. She was working at the magazine, so she would come to my office and we ended up spending more time together. And then, after only a couple of dates, she started talking about the future. I would tune out because I didn't feel anything for her, but I kept hoping maybe eventually I *would* feel something for her. I was starting to think there was something wrong with me. Like maybe the mechanics of my soul had a glitch, because the thing is, I *never* felt a real connection to anyone I dated. Ever. It didn't seem normal. So I tried to force the feelings. She kept telling me she loved me but I wouldn't say anything back. She would get mad about it and we'd have arguments and she'd cry and tell me I was heartless and cold. And I was. And I felt bad about that. Here I was thinking, shit, I'm twenty-six years old and I still can't even *begin* to commit to anyone. I didn't feel anything at all, and I worried about it sometimes. I thought maybe something in me was broken. That maybe I *couldn't* love. So I tried harder, even though I continued to feel nothing. One night, it was after one of our movies had been nominated for five or six Oscars and we'd been out celebrating with a group of people and it had been a good night. She said it again. She told me she loved me and...I said it back. I did. Just to see what it would feel like. I'd never said it to anyone before, ever. Besides Max a couple times when he was a little kid because he needed to hear it from someone, but that's different. My parents weren't really the kind of people who threw those words around, and they both died when we were young. I said it to Vanessa—one time—because she was crying and she was waiting to hear me say it. But you know what? As soon as I said it, I regretted it. It felt wrong. Just completely, totally wrong. I knew I didn't love her. I think I hoped that by *saying* it, it might make me *feel* it. But it did the opposite. It made me want to distance myself even more, because I knew I didn't love her and that I *couldn't* love her. The problem was, once I said it, she believed it. She started talking about getting married. Rings and locations and honeymoons in Paris. I was stupid, really. I should have broken it off earlier but she was so emotional about it and I didn't want to hurt her. I thought maybe I should try harder, that maybe the feelings would come if I gave it some time. But it didn't work. Time didn't help. Nothing helped. And things just got more tense between us because she could detect my total indifference. So I ended it. It might have been a few days before your job interview. Or even the day *of* your job interview, I don't know. It doesn't matter. What matters is that it was over for me a long time ago."

I can't remember ever spilling my guts like this, to anyone. It feels good. Because it's Lexi. Her eyes are all shiny and bright. And there's so much more I still want to tell her. "And then *you* walked in. You just showed up, this *goddess*. This sweet, gorgeous *creature* with these green eyes and your shy, sparked smile. Amazingly, just like that, I *knew*. I knew what had been missing all along. I know what that sounds like, but I think I loved you from that very first second. Your hair was like silky wheat in the sunshine and your smile was the sweetest thing. And I wanted to kiss you so badly I thought I might go insane with it. Absolutely fucking insane. The way you looked at me. I wanted you so much and I could see it there in your eyes, that you did, too. And then once I tasted you, I had to get closer. I needed everything. I mean, *Christ*, I'd never had sex without a condom in my life. I don't think I even cared, deep down, if I got you pregnant. Because then you would have had to stay with me. I mean I wasn't actively *thinking* that but I was already prepared for the consequences. It would mean I could see you again, and stay with you and *be* with you. I'd never committed to anyone as much as I committed to you, right then, and every second since. We were so fucking *hot* for each other but it felt so much deeper than that, too. I was already *all in*, sweetheart. You answered all my questions when you walked into my office that day. I thought: *this. This* is what I want."

Lexi has tears in her eyes. One of them spills and paints a glossy line down her cheek. I wipe it away with my thumb. And I keep going.

"I realized how forced it had all been with the women before you, and how doomed I'd felt. I didn't tell you about Vanessa because it didn't matter. She kept calling, all the time, so I kept my phone turned off. But I needed to check on Max when we were in Hawaii one night, and that's when she called. You were sleeping and I answered it because I wanted to be done with it. So I took the call and it was just as bad as it could have been and I told her again that we were finished. I didn't tell you about that because I didn't want to taint any of the time we had together. Because it *would* have. You know it would have. And it just didn't need to. I should have told you when we got back to L.A. because you were bound to find out eventually, but then there was the whole thing with my other fuck-up, and

I didn't want to make anything worse. I should have told you this morning and warned you about what you'd probably hear about. I'm sorry I didn't. I'm sorry."

I'm prepared to keep going, as long as it takes to convince her. But she's climbing onto me. She takes my face in her hands and she slowly, slowly kisses my lips.

OF COURSE I FORGIVE HIM, if there's anything to forgive. He's no saint, I know this. I don't want a saint. I want Rafe.

I straddle him, kissing his lips. He's in a state that drives me a little crazy, where he surrenders to me, like he's afraid of doing anything else that might hurt me. Just the size of him, the strength, makes this irresistible. He lets me take total control. I lick my tongue into his mouth and he groans.

I feel loose, and reckless. The relief, of hearing his confession, and finding out that what I'd hoped to be true actually *is* true, is quietly extreme. His heartfelt words came at a cost. Everything has a cost. He's proving himself to me. I think he knows how his words affect me. I drink them in, like rain in a desert. I let them soothe away those old fears about being alone. Money doesn't bother me, or cold, even though I'll never go back to it. It's the loneliness that scares me most of all. It's never far from the surface. He so effectively banishes it when he's with me, but the memory leaves an almost unhinged coldness I want—no, *need*—him to fill. My big, warm Rafe knows how to ease away my fears very well.

My nerves are frazzled from the emotions and pace of the day and my body is suddenly voracious, to *feel* him. To lick him and drink him and take him inside. I move slowly, at first. I pull off my dress. I untie the little knot at the back of my neck and my bikini top falls away. Rafe takes my nipple in his mouth, like an offering. He's gentle. I can feel the warm glide of a tear on my cheek but I ignore it. It's just that chink in my soul that lets the sorrow through sometimes, I know this. Rafe's beginning to understand it, too. He gently holds my face. "You're all right, baby girl. I'm here with you. I'll take care of you. I love you."

He's learning. He knows what to say.

I kiss him and he murmurs against my lips. "Let me just hold you, if you're tired. It's all right now. You can sleep."

"No." I don't feel like articulating it in words. I find a button of his shirt and fumble with it. And another. And the hot tears well up and fall.

Rafe carries me to his bed. He pulls the duvet back and sets me against the pillows. He undresses and slides in next to me. He kisses me and his tongue dips into my mouth, lingering briefly. He always seems a little overcome when he does this. Then he kisses away my tears. His mouth moves to my neck. He touches his tongue to my pulse. He kisses a line to my breasts, taking a nipple into his mouth and pulling as he fingers my other nipple. His hands are so strong. I let him hold me and do what I need him to do.

Between bites and licks, as he works his way down my stomach, he murmurs against my skin. "Do you know how much I've missed you today? Do you know how much I worship you?" He holds me down and pulls my bikini bottoms off with his teeth. His fingers brush against my clit and I try not to come yet but he presses his thumb against me as he slides his fingers inside—*god, I'm so wet*—and the orgasm washes through me as sweet, warm, red pleasure. When the waves starts to calm, he lays himself over me. His cock is huge as he pushes into me. Just the feel of him there makes me come again and he rides the spasms, sliding deep. It's excruciatingly good, the big, hot thickness of him as he fills me. I need him there, impaling me with forceful, slippery strokes. He's gentle but not. He's as needy as I am.

Rafe finds my nipple with his mouth and suckles on me very, very gently. He's rock-hard, almost bursting, deeply, thickly inside me as he sucks my breast almost reverentially. The tender suction sends warm channels of pleasure into my body. He feeds that pleasure with the deep, thick drives of his big cock until I come again. My whole body is coming. Bright sparks explode through my body and mind and my inner muscles squeeze him until his cock throbs hotly and fills me with jetting bursts of his hot cum.

His body is heavy. He's in me, on me, around me, everywhere, just where I need him to be. My arms and legs are wrapped around him. My lips are pressed softly against his skin.

"Don't leave me, Rafey," I whisper.

"I'll never leave you."

My last thought, as I drift to sleep, is this: please, please let that be true.

10
___

RAFE

Lexi falls asleep almost instantly. I ease us onto our sides so I won't crush her. Like the lunatic I've become, I don't pull out. I like sleeping like this, inside her, so I can wake up and feel like I've died and gone to heaven. It's a strange feeling, and unprecedented. This need to *stay inside*, to possess her and love her with everything I have. I kiss her lips as I fall asleep.

And when I wake a few hours later, I'm rock-hard, fully wedged inside her snug softness.

I gently smooth her hair back from her face. I kiss her eyelids, her nose, her mouth. I feel her stir. I touch my tongue to hers to see if she'll respond to me. She says my name in a soft, slurred whisper and wraps her arms more tightly around me, snuggling against me as she sighs. She's only half awake. I want to be the kind of dream she doesn't want to wake up from.

"I'm here with you, baby," I whisper, trying to ease her back to the edge of consciousness. Her movements are slow and passive, but my cock is painfully hot and hard. I need her. Again. "Wake up, sweetheart. Feel me."

She half opens her eyes, dreamily, and I groan because the tight, wet silkiness of her feels ludicrously good. I use my fingers to caress her clit. My fingers rub and squeeze and work her pleasure, until her body begins to contract around me—*she's so insanely soft*—and she moans a breathy, kittenish whimper. Her body is rippling, and the squeezing tugs draw out my ecstasy in surging, tumultuous rushes. The pleasure is savage and extreme in a way that seems to change the very alchemy of my soul.

As it always does.

Bonding us. Like we're imprinting each other with the sheer magnitude of our pleasure and our need.

She drifts back to sleep and I watch her face for a while. Then I slip from her body. I get up. I go into the bathroom and wet a washcloth with warm water. I clean the stickiness of our lovemaking from her as she sleeps, before climbing back into bed and holding her in my arms.

But I can't sleep.

My obsession has coiled itself even more tightly around my heart and settled more deeply into the ache in my gut.

I feel only mildly sated. My mind is sliding in crafty directions I have to deliberately steer away from. I could put a couple more executives in place. Run the business from afar. I could take her traveling for months on end, just the two of us. I could design our lives in a way that would make her as reliant on me as it's possible to be.

I won't, of course. I already know she'd draw away from me, in time if not immediately. She doesn't want to feel owned or trapped. I understand all that, of course I do. I learned my lesson. She's not the type who aspires to be kept by a man, unlike so many of the women I've dated.

Maybe that's one of the reasons I'm so drawn to her. She never expects anything from me. She's always surprised, and grateful, for whatever I offer her.

She wears the clothes I bought for her because she doesn't have many others. She wears her ring but doesn't want to show it off. She put all the other pieces of jewelry I gave her back in their original packaging. Like she's planning to give them to someone else. Or save them in case she needs to sell them, for the money.

I understand how a person who comes from poverty thinks, though, because I've been there. It's been a long time since Max and I have had to worry about not having enough food to eat or a warm enough coat to wear, but those little strategies you work through never completely disappear.

I won't crowd her too much or push her too far with my possessiveness, but I want to marry her. Soon. Now. This weekend. I'm thinking about how to convince her to agree to that when I realize it's morning. Somewhere in the middle of my rambling thoughts, I fell asleep.

There's a feather-light touch drawing a line down my shoulder, to my bicep, which she squeezes lightly.

I open my eyes and can only blink at her. She's dazzling. Her eyes are light green, rimmed by those long eyelashes that are dark at the roots and blond at the tips. The light sprinkling of freckles across her nose. Her lips are a shade of pink that's always sort of mind-blowing to me.

"Hi," she says. There's a playful glint in her eyes.

"Hi." I've slept for five solid hours, which is unusual for me. "Marry me on Saturday."

Lexi goes still for a second, then continues drawing her fingertips across my skin, to my chest. "It's pretty quick." She plays my nipple lightly, which makes me flinch and makes my—of course it is—gargantuan beast of a hard-on even more painfully aroused.

Will this ever get easier? Will my lust ever not *feel like it's about to fucking kill me with its intensity?*

"Only three weeks after we first met is...soon."

"I don't care about that." It comes out sounding pissed off, which makes her smile.

"What if..." Her fingers glide lower, over my stomach, down the arrow line of hair. *Fuck.* My cock is a red-hot inferno. My heart is a wild, jazzy animal. "...our feelings for each other start to, you know, cool off..."

"That will never happen."

"You can't know that, Rafe." Her fingers glide along my cock, which rears and throbs and starts to almost spill.

I can't take this. "I *do*. I do know it."

"What if after three or six or ten months...what if our feelings start to change?"

"They won't," I growl, because I'm in agony.

She climbs onto me. "It *is* possible."

She's warm and dewy and my cock fits against her slippery pussy. I am so very close to losing it completely. "No," is all I can manage.

"Where will we do it?" she says.

"Do what?"

"Get married."

She sits up a little and I groan as the head of my cock slides inside her. *Jesus Christ, I can't hold on to this.* "Malibu," I manage to gasp.

"What about flowers?" She writhes gently, almost coyly, taking me deeper.

"Any...kind...you—*oh god*—want."

She leans closer, whispering into my ear. "You're so *big*, Rafey. I think you're about to come." Little minx. She knows exactly what she's doing to me.

"You're right, baby girl."

She kisses me and I'm dizzyingly close to coming. I *am* coming. It's a sure thing. I'm riding the crest of a wave. "I guess I could marry you this weekend," she says. This is a game she's playing, squeezing me with her tight little body. "If I can have white roses."

Oh, fuck. It's too fucking good. "You can...have...white roses."

"What about cake?"

"Yes...cake..."

She arches her back and slides along my length, taking me as deep as she can. "Lemon?" She's getting close too. I can feel it.

"Yeah." I groan. "Lemon."

"I love lemon."

"Me too." I love everything she loves.

She's gently rocking against me. I hold her hips firmly with my hands as I buck into her, thrusting deep. I press my thumb across her clit hard because it's already happening. The rapture is spooling. It bursts out of me in milky, otherworldly surges.

"*Rafe,*" she cries, her voice a soft, rasped chime. "*Oh god, oh god...*"

The clench of her body around my already-jolting climax just about breaks my fucking heart. The throb is whole-bodied, spiritual as well as physical. There's a shattering, connective, astounding intimacy because we're staring into each other's eyes the whole time, or at least as much as we can when we're completely racked with pleasure.

She's watching me, all mussed and sunny with the

pinks and whites and golds that are pure Lexi, as her orgasm washes through her. We kiss. Our tongues dance silkily as the last few ripples die down. "This is out of control," she murmurs. "You're an insatiable beast."

I bare my teeth at her and she laughs. I can only watch her, fascinated by the charmed loveliness of her.

"And you're a magician," I tell her. "I didn't even know I was capable of this kind of stamina."

She smiles and softly bites her lip.

"Don't even pretend to be shy, sweetheart. You know you're a genius at this."

"Am I?" That half-bashful grin.

I touch her hair. The silky strands are so soft they could belong to some mythical creature, like she's just swum up from Atlantis or ridden in on a white unicorn. "I can't wait to marry you, baby girl."

Her smile is still there, still playful, but there's an edge to it. "I'll ask Tess to be my maid of honor. Will Max be your best man?"

"Yes. We'll do it overlooking the beach, if you want. With white roses and lemon cake and lots of candles and a band will play all your favorite songs and we'll get you the prettiest dress you've ever seen."

"A dress," she muses, like she's never considered her own wedding dress before. This is typical of Lexi. When other little girls were busy daydreaming about their fairy-tale weddings and their prince charmings, Lexi was sewing patches over the holes in her clothes or hiding in the dusty lofts of old barns.

Never again. "I'll get Olivia to contact all the top designers and have them send over their best designs. How does that sound? You can get Tess to help you decide."

She pauses. Here we go. "Rafe. That's not necess–"

I put my finger on her lips. "Please. Let me."

She goes still for a second, then holds my finger and pretends to bite it. "Malibu sounds nice."

"It is." I kiss her again. I tell her I love her and I try to be calm and subdued about it because I'm afraid I'll scare her away, if she knew the power behind my passion. *I'm* scared, so I can only imagine how she would feel.

Everything's so perfect when we're alone together. It feels, like perfection tends to do, almost too good to be true.

I'm not naïve enough to think it'll stay this way with no roadblocks or bumps along the way for the rest of time.

I just never expected the bumps to come so fast and so furious.

11

THE ENTIRE FASHION department has gone insane. My wedding dresses have arrived. Twenty-two designers ended up sending four dresses each. Once they heard it was the bride-to-be of Rafe Black, they started arriving, in person, with garments in hand. They've shown up with their racks and their entourages and their equipment, and they're demanding they personally see to each of my fittings.

Olivia is struggling to keep everyone from pushing in to get their designs seen first and all the staff are a little manic. Luckily, Tess didn't have any appointments this week she couldn't cancel—plus this is Downtown, so I really didn't need to ask twice. She dropped everything to be my new assistant, of all things.

"So much for *you* being *my* assistant," she says.

"We can be each other's assistants," I tell her.

Tess has not only risen to the challenge of organizing

an entire department of bossy, over-confident fashion types, she's basically running the place. And her blog suddenly has a hundred thousand new followers.

She holds her iPad, checking the schedule. "Who's with Vera Wang?" she asks the room, using the little microphone that's attached to her mouthpiece. "Vera Wang, you're next."

The Vera Wang team rushes forward, wheeling their laden racks over to where I'm standing. Someone from the Zac Posen contingent almost gets run over and complains, but Tess tells him to stay out of the way and wait his turn.

Tess has everyone obeying her orders, which makes me smile. "You're so in your element," I tell her.

Tess is dressed in a killer light suede skirt, a white frilly shirt and enough (faux) gold accessories to plate the Taj Mahal. At 5'2", Tess could never be described as willowy and will probably never grace a runway, but her hair and make-up are flawless and her flair is undeniable. "You bet your ass I am."

Olivia overhears this and eyes Tess. Olivia seems impressed by the unlikely heroine of the day.

I'm standing here, dressed in an abbreviated pair of lace La Perla panties and a matching push-up bra that's practically see-through—and nothing else—as the Vera Wang team fusses around me. I asked for a privacy screen, or at least something, but Olivia won't hear of it. "They need to be able to *see* you to *fit* you, honey," she informs me. "Besides, most of the men in this room are gay."

Even so, I'm glad Rafe will be busy most of the day.

He managed to get the meeting with the judge moved forward, so he and Max are meeting with their lawyers, the police and also the judge today. It's probably a good thing Rafe can't see me parading around half naked in front of a very busy room full of people. He might go a little crazy (again).

Especially when I glance over and notice someone standing near me, leaning his shoulder against the wall with his hands in his pockets.

Eric Scully.

He has dark blond hair and is tall and sort of lanky. He's wearing a white button-down shirt and blue pants and looks too young to be the executive editor of one of the most cutting-edge companies in the country. I guess he could be described as good-looking, although I'm too used to Rafe, who redefines the word, so everyone else seems a little bland in comparison.

Eric smiles. "Hey, Lexi."

"Uh...hi, Eric."

"Wow, you've really brought in the cool kids. Both Christian and Ralph just asked me if I could get them earlier appointments. They're not used to being kept waiting."

"I don't know why all this is even necessary," I admit.

"Every single one of these dresses is to die for. I would have been happy with any of them."

"It's your wedding dress. You probably want it to be the most glamorous thing you've ever worn."

"I guess so." It's a little strange to be standing here having a conversation with Eric Scully this...on display. Especially after...poker night. I blush at the memory and Eric smiles, like he knows what I'm blushing about, which only makes it worse.

But I'm distracted then by the Vera Wang team, whose hands are on me.

"You need your bra off for this one," someone says and then they proceed to strip me even of that.

I start to fold my arms over my chest but someone *adjusts* me, holding my arms. "We need to you stand still, sweetheart."

Tess leans in and—as subtly as Tess is capable of—says, "I hope Rafe doesn't walk in right now, or heads would be rolling all over the place." She laughs like this is the most hilarious thing in the world.

Eric is still watching me, with an interest that...would definitely piss off his boss.

But then I'm helped into the dress and at least ten people are primping and fussing and pinning the fabric into place.

I look at myself in the full-length mirror in front of me. The dress is definitely the most exquisite thing I've ever worn in my life. It has a fitted lacy bodice that's sewn in a pattern of leaves and flowers that snake around my torso, leaving bare patches between that show my skin, still tanned from Hawaii. There are sequins sewn into the silk, giving the bodice texture and sparkle. The skirt is long and is made entirely of white feathers that have been sewn onto a fine, silk lace. It's fitted in front but has a train with even longer feathers trailing behind it that are white and light yellow and pink and iridescent, giving the whole look an exotic effect.

"You look gorgeous," says Eric Scully. "But then, you looked even more gorgeous without it."

Oh. I'm not sure what to say to that.

"Good luck with the fitting, Lexi," he says. "See you later. We should have a drink when you're finished. Out by the pool."

"Um...sure."

Unlikely. Besides, Rafe will probably be back by then.

Eric smiles and walks away.

One of the women who's adjusting my dress interrupts my thoughts. "I can see why Rafe Black wants to get that wedding ring on your finger as soon as possible, honey. The sharks are circling."

I glance up to see Cole, one of the other guys I met... also on poker night...who's also watching the circus. There are too many people around me for him to get close enough to talk to me, which is probably a good thing. I'm sure everyone on the staff at Downtown is curious about what all the fuss is about, that's all.

"What do you think of this one?" asks Tess.

"It's perfect. This is the one I want."

"Lex, you still have sixty-two dresses to try on."

As flattering as all this might be—I mean, who doesn't want to be treated like a princess once in their life?—it's also exhausting. Rafe woke me up last night, in a good way, but in a way that's left me worn out. Back-to-back orgasms are drugging. They give you an endorphin rush but also a lethargy, once the effect has worn off. When you have as many of them as, well, as *I* happen to have these days, it can be a little exhausting. "Tell them I'll try on only one by each designer. They can choose their best and that's it."

Tess puts her hands on her hips and stares at me. "Look at you, little miss gumption."

"Yes, well, this whole thing is over the top. I can't try on sixty-two more dresses. Twenty more is my limit."

"All right, girl," Tess smiles. She taps her microphone. "Can I have everyone's attention, please. We may already have a winner. And our bride-to-be has decided she'll only try one dress from each remaining designer. So make it a good one."

The room erupts and people start protesting.

Tess speaks loudly, cutting through the noise. "Thank you for your input, but the decision is final. Next up, Ralph Lauren."

Tess watches as the next design team slips the next dress over my head. They're discussing the drape of the fabric and I almost don't hear Tess's question. "Is Max seeing anyone?"

"I don't know. I don't think so. But aren't you dating that new guy—what's his name again?"

"Brandon."

"What about Brandon?"

"He's cute. But let's face it, Max is freaking *scorching*."

I can't argue with that. "Yeah, *and* he's a sweetheart. But he's also…" I don't want to say *on the verge of going to prison*. I'm not sure Max would want me discussing it.

"I kind of picked up on his legal issues the other night, Lex. I was just wondering if you think he might be dating anyone."

I'm not surprised Tess is interested, but don't know if it's a good idea. "He hasn't mentioned anyone. Rafe said he's…well, he used to sleep around a lot."

She laughs. "And? That's hardly unusual, Lex. Just because you never did it doesn't mean other people don't. That's really not a strike against him."

I can guess how it would probably play out. Tess would flirt with him because she's cute and outgoing and fun. He might take her up on it in a casual, I'm-about-to-go-to-jail-so-why-not kind of way. She'd fall head over heels for him because he's an ultra-hot, sensitive bad boy with a heart of gold. What's not to like? But then, he wouldn't return her phone calls because he'd be distracted by, well, *jail* and she'd end up getting her heart broken. It's just a hunch.

"Can you get me his number?"

"I don't have it, Tess. I mean, I can get it, I'm sure, from Rafe, but I think you should be careful, that's all."

"You wouldn't mind, would you, Lexi?"

"Mind?"

"You wouldn't be, like, mad or anything, right?"

"Of course not. Why would I?"

"You just seem very...protective of him. I promise to be gentle."

"It's nothing like that. I just think you should be careful."

"Why? Do you think he's dangerous or something?"

I actually think Max Black is one of the gentlest souls I've ever met. But that soul just happens to be all wrapped up in crazy turmoil and rough edges. "No. I just think dating him would be a wild ride."

"Wouldn't mind finding out." She's smiling, but I'm glad when the next design team swarms around us, ending the conversation.

All the dresses are amazing, but none of them can out-do the Vera Wang.

"Are you sure that's the one you want?" Tess asks.

"If being sure means I want to wear it home, sleep in it and live in it until the end of time, then yes."

"It's a good choice. But you definitely won't be wearing

it...home." There's that word again, which Tess has picked up on. "They'll prepare it for Saturday. Then they'll bring it to wherever the wedding is taking place on Saturday morning to do the final fitting. Where *is* the wedding taking place, by the way?"

"Malibu. Rafe has an estate there."

She rolls her eyes. "Of course he does. Now, what about a bachelorette party?"

"I don't really think it's necessary, Tess. I don't even know who I'd invite." Pathetic, yes, that I've always been too busy studying to concentrate on building friendships, except for Tess, who I'd clicked with the very first time I met her.

"Well, *I* do. I'll throw a little something together for Friday night. You're staying with me that night, anyway. It's bad luck to see the groom on the day of the wedding until you're walking down the aisle, remember? So we'll go out on Friday night and have some fun and you'll stay at my place and then we'll go to Malibu on Saturday morning to get you ready for what's going to be the most kick-ass wedding ever."

I squeeze her hand. "Love you, Tessie. I'm so glad you'll be with me."

She hugs me. "I wouldn't miss it for anything. It's going to be perfect. Don't worry about a thing."

"Tess?"

"Yeah?"

"I'm getting *married* on Saturday. Holy shit."

She laughs and hugs me even more tightly. "To freaking *Rafe Black*. I can't believe how lucky you are."

"I know. It's all just a little crazy, though. My head is spinning."

Her hands are on my shoulders and she's looking at my expression. "You're doing the right thing, sweetie. Don't you second guess a goddamn thing."

"I'm not."

"A million girls would kill to be where you're standing right now."

"I'm not second guessing. It's just...fast."

"Yeah." She smiles. "Remember three weeks ago? When I picked you up from the airport in your glasses and those old baggy jeans and your faded Stanford sweatshirt? Now look at you."

That feels like several lifetimes ago. "It's hard to believe how much has happened since then. I feel like a completely different person."

"You're not, though, Lex. You're still you. Just keep being you and you'll be fine."

"I know. You're right."

"Of course I'm right."

"I'm sorry I went AWOL on you."

"Are you crazy, girl? I would have done the exact same thing. It was a no-brainer."

"I missed you."

"I missed you, too, but I can assure you that if Rafe—or Max—Black happened to offer to sweep *me* off my feet, I wouldn't be looking backwards for anything."

Olivia appears. She walks over and surveys the dress I'm wearing. "So it's the Vera? I couldn't agree more. Oh, and by the way," she turns to Tess. "Tess, is it?"

"Yes. Tess Taylor."

"Tess Taylor, I'd like to offer you a job," says Olivia. "Are you interested in three days a week?"

Tess, for the first time in her life, possibly, is speechless.

"You can still run your blog," Olivia adds. "I'm sure we can offer you an employment package that will be exceptionally generous. Do you have a minute to talk in my office?"

"Go ahead," I tell Tess, when she gives me a searching look, making sure I can handle things on my own for a few minutes. "I'm fine. This is the last one anyway."

Tess goes off with Olivia and I'm—finally—stripped of the last dress of the day.

I put my white cotton dress back on and check my phone. Five o'clock on the dot, and what do you know, Eric Scully is walking toward me.

"Ready for that drink?"

"Actually, a drink sounds amazing. I feel like I need one."

12

It's just a drink.

I don't need permission to have one drink with a work colleague.

Besides, Tess will probably join us. Maybe even Olivia. And Rafe and Max, when they're finished, and we can all hang out and pretend like my little meltdown on poker night never happened.

We go out to the pool area where there's a bar and tables. Eric chooses a table for two. "What'll you have?"

"A glass of champagne. Thanks." It's what I've become used to drinking, with Rafe.

"I'll get us a bottle."

Eric comes back with an ice bucket, the opened bottle and two glasses. He starts pouring the champagne and I'm suddenly kind of regretting this. There are other people around, swimming, drinking, working, but this secluded little table under a palm tree with just the two of us feels a little too...intimate. I look over to see if Tess and Olivia might be coming out to join us but there's no sign of them.

"I'm glad you're getting some time to settle in here at Downtown without your bodyguard," Eric says.

At first I think he's talking about Olivia. "My bodyguard?"

He smiles. "He doesn't let you out of his sight much, does he? I was beginning to wonder if you're ever allowed out of this building. I imagine you crave a little fresh air every now and then."

I'm not sure why Eric would say something like that. Is this him being kind? Or...something else?

"I want to confess something to you." Eric clinks his glass against mine and takes a sip. "I have a Plan B."

"What kind of Plan B?"

"After poker night, my job feels a little less secure than it used to."

God, why does he have to bring that up? What does he want me to do...apologize? My face gets hot again. "I'm sorry to hear that."

This is awkward, for me at least, but he smiles. "I've started a new company. It's just a sideline at this point, but it's gaining some momentum. I thought it would be a good idea to have a place to crash land, in case my head happens to be on the chopping block."

As much as I hate to think Eric's predicament might be

my fault, I can't really worry about it. Technically it's actually...Rafe's fault. "I'm sure it isn't. You must be very good at your job. Downtown is thriving."

"I like to think so. But there's plenty of talent out there. I'm thoroughly expendable, and Rafe knows it."

"That can't be true."

He's watching me as he takes another sip of his drink. "You have the greenest eyes. You really are incredibly beaut—"

"Eric." This was clearly a mistake.

He smiles again, more widely this time. His teeth are that shade of white that looks borderline unnatural. "Sorry. I'll behave, I promise. I just wanted to point out that you do have choices, you know."

"I don't know what you mean."

"I've been working for Downtown for three and a half years," he continues. "Some healthy competition is always a good thing for a company. The idea's been forming for a year or so now, and, well, recent events have spurred me into action." I try not to think too closely of the recent events he's referring to. "I found a space and I've just hired my first employee." Eric Scully's eyes hold mine. I'm really not sure why he's telling me all this. "I'd appreciate it if you kept this information to yourself for the time being, Lexi. Just until I know for sure one way or the other."

"Um, sure, but maybe you shouldn't be—"

"Please. Just hear me out. This is probably out of line,

all things considered, but keep it tucked away for a rainy day, just in case. I've seen your résumé and I definitely have a job available for you. If you ever need it."

I stare at him. "Eric...I really don't know why you'd offer that."

"I know what you're thinking. You're thinking: I don't need a job. I *have* a job. I have a company to learn and a fiancé to obey and a big fat expense account to work my way through."

"Eric. Please—"

He puts his hands up in a don't-shoot-me apology. "Sorry, sorry. But keep it in mind, in case you ever need to. Sure, you don't need it *today*. But some day, you might. Consider it an ace in the hole, to fall back on." *Really? Another poker reference?* I'm starting to get immune to them at this point but I can feel fresh heat on my face. Again. "I've worked for Rafe for a while now. I know how over-bearing he can be. You might want an alternative at some point. That's all I'm saying."

Eric Scully has some nerve. "That won't happen."

"Probably not," he says. "But I just wanted to let you know the offer's on the table if you ever need it."

He thinks my marriage to Rafe won't work. He thinks Rafe will drive me away by being too...Rafe.

"I won't need it. You're wrong, by the way."

I hear footsteps behind me and turn. It's Rafe. And Max.

"Wrong about what?" says Rafe.

They pull chairs over and sit on either side of me. Rafe sits between me and Eric.

Rafe notices the look on my face, and the blush on my cheeks. He glances at Eric, then back at me. "Everything okay?"

My heart skips a beat, both from the conversation with Eric, and from Rafe's sudden nearness. I forget when I'm apart from him how stunning he is. How electric he makes everything feel. How broad his shoulders are in his exquisitely-cut suit. How his black hair lightly curls at the tips where it almost touches his collar, slightly windswept like he's just driven in from some wild, idyllic ranch in Montana where the rivers are so clean you can drink them. There's something so tantalizingly rugged about him, like a pirate king whose look screams *I'll give you the hottest sex of your life and make all your wildest fantasies come true.*

I happen to know this is true.

And I'm relieved. He's here now.

Eric's wrong about him. Rafe has given me all the assurances I need. I know he's aggressive and protective and even overbearing sometimes. I *like* him that way. Screw Eric and his unfounded predictions and his goddamn Plan B.

"Wrong about what?" Rafe says again. He's reading the lingering vibe.

"Wrong about the dress he thought I was going to

choose," I bluff. Eric very definitely *would* lose his job if Rafe knew what Eric had just offered me.

Rafe smiles. "You chose one?"

"Yes. It's perfect."

"I can't wait to see it," he says softly. I can sense a brimming energy in him. I can only hope it's an energy that *keeps its cool* because there are definitely a few sparks flying.

I glance at Max, who also notices. He's watching Rafe.

Max looks worn out, like he needs a good night's sleep and someone to tell him everything's going to be okay.

Which may or may not be true.

"How'd it go today?" I ask him.

"The sentencing is tomorrow," he says, taking a sip of my champagne. "Ask me then. I want you there, by the way. I need all the moral support I can get."

"Sure, Max. Of course I'll be there."

Olivia and Tess join us and a waiter brings more chairs and serves us two more bottles of champagne. Olivia makes a big production about Tess being Downtown's newest employee.

Rafe's eyebrows lift. "Wow. That's great."

Tess—I can't help but notice—chooses the chair next to Max's.

"Tess had those designers lined up like it was a military regimen," Olivia gushes. "It was fabulous. You have no idea how hard it is to do that. I hired her on the spot."

Max clinks his glass against Tess's. "Congrats."

Tess blushes bright pink and practically melts into her chair. "Thanks, Max."

Olivia sits in the chair next to Eric's. "The only people *not* following Tess's orders were the Downtown staff," she continues, winking at Eric, and what I'm thinking is: *Please don't go there. Please don't go there.*

But go there she does. I already know Olivia loves drama. If she continues down *this* road, though, she might get a lot more drama than she bargained for. The kind of drama we *really* don't need right now.

"Is that right?" says Rafe, curious.

"We had to shoo them back into their offices," Olivia continues. "Lexi sure knows how to wow a crowd. The dress is absolutely to die for, by the way. I can't fault her taste. It fits her like a second skin. Isn't that right, Eric?"

Is she intentionally trying to escalate this?

After a pause, Eric replies, "Sure is."

Not a good response, actually. They don't seem to know Rafe as well as I do. They don't seem to see that his composure is walking a knife's edge, already.

Rafe's fist clenches. I put my hand on it. "Maybe we should go upstairs," I say to him, keeping my tone light.

Max can read the writing on the wall as clearly as I can. And Rafe won't let it go. He's glaring at Eric. "How do *you* know what the dress looks like?"

"Oh, Eric happened to be there for part of it," Olivia

rambles, "actually quite a *lot* of it, not that he was the only one." She's either completely unaware or fishing for a reaction, I can't quite tell. "Lexi had to be in the open fitting area, of course, since there were so many designers clambering to get their dresses seen."

"So..." Rafe is processing. "...*everyone* was watching you get undressed." *Including Eric*, I can practically hear him thinking.

Max still has a faint bruise around his eye from his recent pummeling from Rafe. Maybe he's trying to spare Eric the same fate. "Sounds like Lexi was choosing the right dress to *marry* you in on Saturday, Rafe."

Rafe is still staring at Eric. And he seems to read something in his expression. "Tell me what you were talking to Lexi about just now. When I interrupted you."

Olivia clinks her drink against Tess's. She doesn't seem to realize the match she's lit.

I try to brush Rafe's question breezily aside. "I already told you. Come on, we should get going."

But Rafe isn't budging. His arm feels like it's made of hot, newly-forged steel.

And Eric seems to understand that his time at Downtown has just run out. "I told her I had a Plan B, that I'm handing in my resignation and that if she's ever looking for a job that isn't under your thumb I have one for her."

Why the hell would he say that? Does he have a death wish or something?

When Rafe stands up, so does Max.

And so does Eric.

Oh no.

Rafe grabs the front of Eric's shirt with his fist. His voice is very low and very direct when he says, "*Stay the fuck away from her.*"

A few people at the other tables are starting to turn.

It doesn't help when Eric says, "She was enjoying some freedom, that's all. No harm done."

"You're fucking fired," Rafe growls, still holding the front of Eric's jacket.

With effort, Max removes Rafe's hand from Eric's shirt, patting it back into place. "We can take that through the proper channels, Rafe. Let's see if we can avoid prison sentences for both of us, shall we? Calm the fuck down."

Max somehow manages to pull Rafe away from Eric before things get totally out of hand.

"I want you out of here within the hour or I'll fucking remove you myself," Rafe fumes.

Max and I do our best to pull Rafe away. Max is murmuring words like "aggravated assault" and "jail time," which seem to—just—be enough to keep Rafe from crossing a line.

"My offer stands, Lexi," Eric calls after me. It takes all of Max's powers of persuasion to keep Rafe from lunging at Eric. I'm suddenly glad Max is so...freaking...beefed up. He looks like he's been working out non-stop. I guess pumping iron could be a good form of stress release, who knows. We get to Rafe's private elevator and as soon as the doors open, Max pushes Rafe gently into it. "Good luck with that," he says to me wryly. "I'm going home. I'll see you two in the morning."

"Thank you, Max. See you tomorrow. Try to get some sleep."

The doors slide closed and Rafe and I stand there in stony silence for a few seconds. I'm reminded again how big he is in this confined space. His fury is radiating off of him like waves.

Haven't we evolved past this? He's still acting like we're all living in caves and dragging our knuckles and going ape-shit whenever our territory is encroached on.

"You really didn't need to overreact like that. Nothing happened."

He spears me with a look. "*Some*thing happened. He *wants* you, that's what happened. He offered you a fucking *job*. That's not *nothing*, Lexi."

"Well, *I* don't want *him*, more importantly. And I'm obviously not going to accept the job, am I? It was nothing I couldn't handle, Rafe. You didn't need to go all caveman about it."

He glares at me. "Of course I'm going to go *caveman* about other people salivating all over *my* gorgeous fiancée! Especially *him*."

The elevator doors slide open and I storm into his apartment. He follows me.

"You don't need to try to control everything all the time, Rafe! And you shouldn't need to. I could have handled it. Why do you get so worked up all the time?"

"*Worked up*? Maybe I'm *worked up* because I've spent the entire day begging some old battle axe of a judge not to lock my brother up for ten years, only to then find my fiancée sharing a private drink with *Eric fucking Scully*, who was trying like hell to get you into bed while meanwhile feeding you lines about how overbearing I am as he offered you a job! How do you *expect* me to react to that, Lexi?"

"He wasn't trying—"

"Of course he was! You have no idea the effect you have on men. *I* do. And there's no way in hell I can sit back and be all blasé about it, even if I wanted to!"

This alpha male schtick takes some getting used to. After a lifetime of quiet libraries and being completely independent and also basically hiding myself away from the collective attention of humankind, it's a little intense. "I'm not asking you to be *blasé*. I'm *asking* you to trust me! You don't get to decide what I do or who I do it with. Or how I choose to handle whatever happens next. Whether you like it or not, you're going to have to get used to me doing things that don't always fit into the parameters of what you can control!"

Rafe's glaring at me. His fists are still balled and, amazingly, so are mine. It could have been almost comical, if it wasn't so infuriating. "My 'parameters'"—using air quotes—"are an obliterated pile of rubble at this point."

"No kidding, Rafe. God. You act like a crazy person. I know what all that looked like, and yes, what he said was inappropriate, but you can't go around beating people up all the time! That's not a solution. You're out of control."

He spears me with another look.

"I don't need your permission to have a drink with a work colleague," I remind him.

"I know that!" Rafe runs a hand through his hair, making it stick up. "I also know that this isn't just *any* work colleague, and that the minute he saw you he was willing to throw away almost four years of a stellar career and one of the best jobs in the city, just for a chance to get close to you." There's a note of agony weaved into his rage. "I do trust *you*, Lexi. But I don't trust Eric Scully as far as I can fucking throw him."

It's his despair that seeps into me. Rage is a new one for me. But despair is something I can relate to. "Nothing happened, Rafe. And nothing was going to happen. I love *you*. I'm about to *marry* you. Isn't that enough?"

These words affect him, I can see that.

"Do you think maybe we need a little more time?" I say gently. "To figure all this out?"

He scoops me into his arms and starts carrying me into his bedroom.

"*Rafe*. Put me down."

He sets me carefully on his bed and kneels down in front of me. He looks anguished. "Please don't say that."

"I can't marry you if you keep trying to control me—and everyone else—all the time. It won't work."

He holds my face with his hands and they're hot. "Lexi. I'm not trying to *control* you, can't you see that? I just don't want some lecherous asshole trying to steal you away from me. That's what he was trying to do, don't you see? Of course I'm going to react. You're *mine*. I'll do whatever I have to do to keep you safe."

He's a big, buff, over-possessive alpha and nothing's ever going to change that. I don't *want* to change that. But I'm still figuring out how to handle it. "I love that you love me this much, Rafe. I do. But you have to trust me to do the right thing. I want *you*. Not Eric Scully or anyone else. You have to let me handle my own life. Without threatening everyone who talks to me."

Rafe tucks a strand of my hair behind my ear and his touch is so gentle it's hard to believe this is the same man that, only minutes ago, had to be restrained from beating one of his employees to a bloody pulp. "Okay."

"Okay?"

"Yes. I'll do whatever you tell me to do. Whenever you tell me to. Anything."

"You don't have to do *whatever* I tell you to do. I'm not asking you to blindly obey me. I'm just asking you to trust me. I would have walked away within the next minute if you hadn't shown up, anyway. You didn't need to go ballistic. Again."

"I know," he murmurs into the silk of my dress, grabbing handfuls with his hands. "I'll try harder. Just please don't say you won't marry me, Lex. *Please.* I'll make it up to you. Just tell me what to do and I'll do it. Please don't push me away, baby girl. I can do it. I'm getting better already."

I smooth a strand of his hair back into place. "Are you?"

"All the time. It's just that the changes are incremental. You can't always see them but they're there. Definitely."

I laugh a little. "Sure they are. You're crazy, you know that?"

"Crazy doesn't even begin to describe how much I worship you." He kisses my lips softly. His hands rove under my dress. He lays me back on the bed and crouches over me, like a big cat. His hands are so warm, his mouth so hungry. He moves lower, pushing my dress up and kissing my stomach, my thighs.

"You're incorrigible," I tell him. My panties are already wet from the way his fingers are rubbing and pushing the silk aside. He's so strong, so insistent.

"In a good way, though, right?"

His tongue licks into me as his fingers glide across my

clit. His warm, hot mouth latches and pulls in a perfect rhythm. *He's so damn good at that.*

"In the worst way," I gasp, but I'm already coming.

135

13

———

I WAKE IN THE NIGHT. I feel for him in the darkness but his side of the bed is empty.

I get up, and wrap a silk robe around me, tying it at the waist. "Rafe?"

He's not in the kitchen or the living room.

Using the code, I let myself into his office and carefully push the door open a crack.

I can hear him talking to someone. I can tell by his tone he's angry. Agitated. He's making an effort to placate whoever he's talking to.

"I'm not listening to that kind of bullshit. You don't know anything." A pause. "I know you don't want to accept it but you *have* to," he says gruffly. "It's *over*, Vanessa. I don't know what else I can say to you to get you to understand."

So that's who he's talking to.

"*No.* Meeting with you won't change my mind.

Goddamn it. There's nothing else to say. I'm trying to be as kind as I can about this, but this is getting way out of hand. I'm—" Another long pause. Rafe sighs heavily. "Look, crying's not going to—*No*. You *have* to accept it. *Please*, just fucking deal with it. It's over."

I think about leaving him to it. Maybe he wants privacy, but he feels my presence. He turns and sees me. He motions for me to come in.

I walk over and sit on his desk. His clenched fist is resting on his thigh.

He's worried about how I might react, I can read that in his eyes. Vanessa's voice is shrill through the phone as she cries and pleads with him.

"Look," he says brusquely. "I have to go now. I've told you how it is. Please just accept that. And please—for the last time—stop contacting me. I won't reply again. There's nothing more to say. Goodbye, Vanessa."

Rafe ends the call, turns off his phone and places it on his desk.

"Hi." His voice is dark-edged, unsettled.

"Hi."

He's in a volatile mood. I've seen it many times before, and it's there now, in the dark glint of his eyes. He stands up. He looks huge, hulking, strong. He's wearing only a pair of jeans. The play of his muscles, taut and powerful, is riveting. If I didn't know him so well and trust him so implicitly, I might feel intimidated.

I concentrate on his beauty. The light sneer of his mouth. "I suppose you're mad at me, are you?"

"No."

"She keeps saying she has something she wants to tell me in person. But I'm done."

"I heard."

"She's...making threats. About hurting herself. That's the only reason I called her back."

"Is she all right?"

He contemplates me. "You want to know if she's all right." It's not a question. "She's insane, but still alive, apparently. I'm not trying to be heartless. I'm just over it."

He stares down at me, as though expecting me to challenge him.

"I'm not mad at you, Rafe. You had to make sure she's okay. That's understandable."

"I've done my best to let her down easy, but she's fighting me every step of the way. She's insisting we meet, but I refused." His expression is agitated, almost aggressive. "You're not going to have a big meltdown over it? Or accuse me of secretly talking to my ex every time you leave the room?"

"Why would I?"

"Because every other woman I know would."

Vanessa is clearly frustrating him beyond belief. Maybe more than I realized. "I guess the obvious answer to that is that...I'm not every other woman."

He's still glaring at me, as though he can't believe I'm as calm as I am.

"You already explained it to me, Rafe. I believe you. I trust you."

This information seems to flick some invisible switch in Rafe. He gets very quiet but his body is practically humming with tension. "You trust me," he finally says.

"Yes."

"I don't think you do."

I'm not sure what he means by this. "Why would you say that?"

"You keep things from me."

A tiny wash of...that old feeling I get when I think about my past ices through my veins. I want to steer him away from this topic. The fact is, I *do* keep things from him. We both know this. We've kind of dealt with it. I thought he'd accepted that part of me. The hidden-away part.

We sit there in silence for a while, and his aggression is suddenly gone. He's not going to push me, I realize. And it's this realization—of his patience and his compassion— that makes me want to give him what he wants, more than if he'd argued or somehow tried to force it.

He told me the story about his time with Vanessa. He gave me honesty. And it helped. So much that, now, I don't feel like there's any reason to doubt him.

"You're right," I admit. "I do keep things from you."

He gives me a look that's so sympathetic and

connective, it makes my heart feel heavy with love for him. He *gets* me, like no one ever has, simply by *wanting* to get me. For wanting to *feel* everything I feel. "You'll share with me when the time is right for you, I know that."

"It's just not something I like to talk about, Rafe."

"It helps to share it. It...it helped Max to talk about it. I just want you to know that I'll be careful with you. When you're ready."

My eyes sting. *My Rafe.* He always knows how to spear into my emotions like he's got a radar for their bullseye. There's no hiding anything from him. With anyone else, this would scare me. With him, it gives me hope. "Thank you."

He smiles gently. "Do you want to go back to bed now?"

"Yeah."

He takes my hand. "So we're all good with...the Vanessa thing?"

"As I said, I trust you."

I let him pull me by the hand and we walk back into his apartment, to his bedroom. We climb into bed. He wraps his arms around me and the only sound in the room is of the hum of luxury. Of climate control and expensive, cocooned warmth.

He's holding me close in his bear-grip. Long-buried abysses in my soul pulse in a dark, painful rhythm.

"You're safe," he whispers in the darkness. "I'm here for you in whatever way you need me to be. I'm yours."

There's an unfamiliar looseness in me. Like his fierce love has opened a door somewhere inside me, just a crack, letting light in. "Thank you for being the kindest person I know, Rafey."

"I don't know how kind I am. But I do know I love you to the point of insanity."

I smile. "I agree you're kind of crazy sometimes."

"Can't help myself. You're everything I never even knew I wanted, times around a quadrillion. It's a little intense."

After a while, I say, "Where should I start?"

"At the beginning."

So I do. I take a breath and Rafe's warm fingers weave through mine. I start telling him things I've never told anyone. "My mother was always unstable. Just...broken. All because my father left her. Which is hard, of course. But I could never quite understand why that had to ruin everything for us and our entire lives. We had each other, that was something. But it was never enough for her. I couldn't seem to fill that void that my father left when he walked out on us. She was completely snowed under by her heartbreak. I wondered what kind of person would do that to his wife and his unborn baby. I wondered about that a lot. How could he do that to her? To us? Why didn't he want to know me, his own child? Who just walks away like that and never looks back? She never, ever recovered from that. She existed in this grief-stricken haze that tainted everything."

I stop and Rafe doesn't push me. His patience feels like a safety net. So I keep going.

"One day, years later, when I was ten, she told me she'd met someone. At first I couldn't believe the changes in her. In all the time I'd known my mother, she'd never been happy. And suddenly, she almost was. He moved in with us soon after, and my mother was excited. She even cut back on the drinking for a while, at the beginning. When he moved in, it felt like maybe we were finally going to have... a family."

I pause and Rafe traces the wing of my eyebrow with his finger. He's listening. Waiting for whatever I can give, and nothing more. His quiet encouragement is giving me courage.

"Our house was almost like a normal house for the first few months or so. It was cleaner than it had ever been. She even cooked and we'd eat at the table. Once, she even picked some flowers and we talked and it was nice. Different. But then the newness started to wear off, as I guess it tends to do. They'd argue sometimes. And then one day he hit her. Just once, but it took a long time for the black eye to fade. She started drinking again. Just a little at first but then she started sinking right back in to her old habits. She'd miss things. Like the way he looked at me when her back was turned. She'd pass out on the couch and...I think he realized that no one would stop him. He got bolder. He would say things to me. At first I tried to ignore it. But it got worse. I didn't know what the words meant. But I did understand that he was going to hurt me."

I focus on the warmth of Rafe's hand squeezing mine.

"I didn't want to leave my mother. I was afraid for her. I tried to tell her, but she just wouldn't listen. I knew I couldn't save us both. I knew I had to leave."

"It's good you did," Rafe says softly.

His hands are warm, the burn in his eyes a deep shade of blue in the darkness.

"It was a relief, once I got out. I was free, and safe from what might have been. But then there were all the other dangers. The cold. The fear of being caught and found by someone else who might be just as bad or even worse. The loneliness was almost as bad as the fear. Maybe even worse. I wondered if I'd ever escape from either one of those feelings. They were so big. My whole life was consumed by being lonely and being scared. For a very long time."

"And now you're here with me. I'll make sure you're never lonely or scared again. I promise you."

We're silent for a while, as he wipes my tears away.

"Keep going," he says gently.

I find that, amazingly, I can. "The barn was warm. The animals were like...friends. I liked the sounds they made. I lived there for a few months. I got up with the sun and snuck out and tried to clean myself up in the creek and then I'd go to school. But one night I dropped one of my mittens off the side of the loft. The farmer's son found it. It was dark. He came up the ladder to the loft with his flashlight to see if anyone was there. I was so terrified he would find me. I hid with my backpack behind a pile of hay. I thought he'd hear my heartbeat, it was beating so hard. I thought he'd find me, but somehow he didn't. As soon as he was gone, I left. I found a chicken coop. It was small but so was I. Until they got suspicious and it just felt too risky. Then I found a place under a bridge near the school. There was a cave. It was cold but dry. I lived in that cave for two months, until my teacher noticed how dirty my clothes were. I tried to wash them in the river, but it was harder to do in the winter."

Rafe murmurs soft words, and I keep going. I want to get it all out so I can be done with it once and for all.

"Once they realized, the social workers could see that my mother was in no state to take care of me. They put me in foster care, and it was the same thing all over again. The men would look at me, and say things. I would run before they could act on the threats in their eyes, because I was expecting them. I'd seen them before. It happened so many times I lost count. By then I knew how to hide. I got good at it. I got good at stealing food and clothes and blankets. I got better at fooling my teachers. I found a library that was open late."

I take a breath and then exhale, and it feels like a beginning. *Let it go.* That's exactly what I'm starting to do. I've blocked these ghosts from my thoughts for so long it feels strange now and somehow wildly therapeutic to tell the story. To let Rafe share the burden.

"I'm lucky, I realize now," I tell him. "I escaped every single one of them, just in time. I got out before they could do...whatever it is they might have done. But I paid the price. I lived rough and I lived alone. For a very long time."

"You've had a terrible time, Lexi, but you're not damaged," Rafe says, and his voice is so steady and so sure I know I can believe him. "You can put it behind you and heal if you let yourself."

"I am healing. Because of you." I pause, taking a minute to think about how to say what I want to say. "You know how you said when you met me, on that very first day, you felt a connection to me you never even thought was possible, because you'd never experienced anything like that before? Well I did too, Rafe. I felt safe with you in a way that didn't even make sense." I look over at him and he's still watching me. "I guess our reaction to each other was...unusual."

"We're meant to be together and we could both feel that."

"I'm glad you know now, Rafe. I don't want to have secrets from you."

He cups my face with his hand. "We all have baggage

and secrets and memories we wish we could forget. None of us are unscathed by life. What I want to do with your baggage is unpack it and rearrange it. We'll throw away the things you don't need any more and replace them with new stuff. Fun memories and happy ones. That's my job. That's all I want to do. If you'll let me."

How does he always know the exact thing I need to hear at the exact moment I need to hear it? He really does have a knack. "I'll let you if you let me."

There it is: his slow smile. "Deal."

After confessing all that, I feel weirdly *light*, like years of dull weight have been lifted and my peripheral vision is no longer black and hidden, but new and somehow sparked.

I kiss him. Slowly. Tenderly. "Close your eyes, Rafey."

He's watching me, trying to interpret my request. I wait for him to obey, which, after a few seconds, he does. His eyes close. It's strange. Rafe and I share a bond that's incredibly tactile. That was our very first connection, a physical one. Like magnets that can't resist each other's pull. This meandering, forging love grew out of a wild, uninhibited lust. We can communicate with our bodies, at times, what we can't always put into words. I love him. I feel so lucky to have found him. And I need the comfort of his touch as much as the comfort of his understanding. I kiss him again, taking more. I press myself against him. I want to feel all of him. I want to get as close to him as it's possible to do.

"Lexi, baby, are you sure? You—" He draws in a sharp breath when I move a certain way, so his hot, rigid cock slides against my softness.

I love the textures of his big, hard body, dusted with hair and quilted with ridge upon ridge of muscle. The lingering upheaval of my emotions is driving me in desperate directions as I grip him harder.

His strong hands are guiding me, holding me down. He can feel the frenzy in me, and he uses his strength and his murmured words to calm me. "It's all right. I'll give you everything you need. I'll take such good care of you. Let me in, that's my girl. I'll make you feel so good."

Rafe lays me back and slides his massive cock into me, slowly, slowly, making sure I'm wet enough to take him, that he's not hurting me, easing himself inside. I whisper love words in his ear as he forces the dazzling pleasure higher in a warm surge, until the rhythm brings me to a shattering peak that works him in squeezing tugs until he growls and finds his own surging release.

After, we lay there for a long time, replete and completed, awed by the beauty of this sublime connection.

14

RAFE

I SHOWER AND GET DRESSED, letting Lexi sleep as long as I can. She's tired. We stayed up half the night, working through things that needed to be said.

She's suffered, from the kind of trauma you don't get over without working through it, laying it out and dealing with it in a way that makes sense. We can look into therapy down the line if she'll agree to it. The first step is admitting you've been hurt, and realizing it's not your fault.

I knew she'd never trust me completely if she couldn't be honest with me. Somehow, I broke through. And now I can begin to help her heal. I know only too well how a person can carry that shit around with them for a lifetime, thinking they fucked up when it wasn't them at all. When they'd only been a child who needed love and instead got hell.

I know all about it.

"Lexi." I kiss her lips. "Time to wake up, baby."

The meeting with the lawyers that will decide Max's sentence starts at nine o'clock. I'm still optimistic we'll get away with a whopping payout and some community service, but it could go either way. While Lexi's in the shower, I call Max.

He picks up on the first ring. "Hey."

"Did you get any sleep?"

"Nope. You?"

"Not much. You're wearing a suit, right?"

"No, I'm dressed head to toe in leather. I'm not a complete fucking imbecile, Rafe."

"Good. Just checking."

It isn't hard to sense his mood. Gone is the carefree player. He's staring down the barrel of some serious time, and the reality of his situation is definitely starting to sink in.

"We'll get you through this, Max, whatever happens. We've got plenty of money to throw around, so our chances are good. Let's just wait to hear what the judge decides before we start panicking."

He's unflappably morose. "Sure thing, brother."

I could say, *You got yourself into this mess, now you have to deal with the consequences of your actions*, like some asshole. I've tried plenty of times to get Max to toe the line, but it doesn't make a difference. He pretty much does the opposite of what he's told to do, and always has. It's just his way. So instead I just say, "We'll meet you in the lobby of the courthouse at eight thirty."

"Lexi's coming, right?"

"Yes." There's something sort of endearing about the way he's begun to rely on her. Max has had plenty of women in his life, but, like me—until now, at least—there's never been anyone who stuck. He's become attached to the way Lexi genuinely cares about him. Not his money or his cars or his motorcycles or his looks. Just him. We've already worked through my jealousy. Now, I find I *like* that the only two people I really care about in this world genuinely feel for each other.

"I'll see you soon, then." He ends the call.

When we arrive at the hearing, Max is already there—looking as respectable as I've ever seen him look—and the proceedings get underway promptly at nine o'clock.

Apparently, the prosecution has done some thinking over the past two days because the vibe has changed from one of blood to one of money. Maybe it's their tactic. All week they've issued threats to nail us so firmly to the wall that Max wouldn't see the light of day for years to come. Maybe they wanted to scare us, to get us thinking about how much we'd actually prefer to give them millions of dollars than to put Max through incarceration and all its ongoing, nightmarish side-effects.

The lead prosecutor is a swish dickhead named Rick Owens who has a reputation for annihilating rich businessmen who take liberties with inside information. People exactly like Max. Owens is in full-on attack mode. "Our clients have decided they'll consider taking a monetary settlement rather than pushing for jail time for the defendant. Their out of pocket costs are roughly equivalent to five point five million dollars. After costs and damages they ask for a settlement of six million dollars."

Max exhales a low curse only Lexi and I can hear. It's a huge amount of money. But it could be a lot fucking worse.

He's pulled off the clean-cut look fairly impressively. He looks both rich and wholesome, definitely not his usual style. You'd never know by looking at him that he's both a criminal and a renegade. Then again, we wouldn't be here if he wasn't at least one of the two. He's also devastatingly handsome, a detail I can only hope will work in his favor. The judge is an older woman, probably in her mid-sixties, who's clearly at least ten years beyond being either charmed or impressed by anything besides justice. Still, it can't hurt that he looks like he just stepped out of the pages of GQ.

We'll soon find out one way or the other.

The room is entirely silent. The judge contemplates Max. She takes off her reading glasses and sets them aside. "Mr. Black," she says to him. "Do you regret what you've done?"

"Yes, ma'am," Max says earnestly. "I've caused a lot of trouble for a lot of people." Max looks at me, then back at the judge. "People I care about. I'm going to do my best to make it up to them." I don't think I've ever heard my brother sound more miserable, or more sincere. "Once I get out."

The judge continues. "In light of the prosecution's statement, I'd be willing to forego a prison sentence, on two conditions. The defence will pay Mr. Owens' clients reparations in the amount of six million dollars. And Mr. Maximilian Black will be placed under house arrest for a period of three months, effective immediately. He'll be fitted with an electronic device to track his movements and his communications. He will be permitted to go to his home and to his place of employment. According to the information you've given, Max Black's home is directly around the corner from his workplace. He may walk, he may drive, he may stop for the occasional cup of coffee, but he may not travel off course from the direct route between the allocated locations defined in his sentence. If he violates the terms of this house arrest, he'll be immediately sentenced to a three-year prison sentence with no possibility of parole." She gives Max a soulful but steely look. "I'm letting you off the hook this time, Mr. Black, assuming you can meet the cost of reparations. But I will not be so generous again. Next time you'll be prosecuted to the full extent of the law. Do you understand these terms?"

"Yes." Max's voice sounds rasped and doomed. Six million dollars is a lot of money. If I were to ask Max the question, I know he thinks it's more than his freedom is worth. I disagree. *This* is what I've worked my fucking guts out my entire goddamn life to be able to do: to save him, always, when he needs to be saved.

The judge puts her glasses back on. "I'll now give you a few minutes to consult with your legal team about how you would like to respond."

I stand up. "That won't be necessary, your honor. I'll pay the six million dollars immediately. And Max is more than willing to respect the terms of his house arrest. We accept the terms."

Max stares up at me and his expression haunts me. It reminds me of all the hardship he's seen. All the scars he still carries.

"Fine." The judge studies me, but I detect a note of what might be subdued relief, as though she's been silently rooting for Max's happy ever after. "Once you've signed the paperwork and handed over your check," she says, "and your brother has met with the supervising authority to be fitted with his tracking device, you're free to go."

"One more thing," I add. The judge glares at me. "I'm getting married at my house in Malibu on Saturday after-noon. Max is supposed to be my best man. I wondered if you'd allow him one night out of...the zone. If he agrees not to leave the Malibu premises on the night and to return home by eight a.m. the following morning."

The judge doesn't react at first, but her gaze slides from me, to Lexi, to Max. Lexi's sitting between us. Max and Lexi are both stunning-looking people, with a bruised vulnerability that sort of clings to them. It's hard to tell, but I get the feeling the judge sees it too: the decency in them, the innocence lost through no fault of their own.

"Permission granted."

15

RAFE

MAX GOES BACK to his office for a while to pack up his stuff.

I call him to tell him we've decided to go get a drink somewhere in the confines of his "zone."

"I didn't do it, by the way," he says.

"Didn't do what?"

"Leak the info."

"What do you mean?"

"I mean someone framed me. Someone hacked into my account and sent the emails. I didn't give out any insider information. I'm clean as a goddamn whistle."

I can't believe what I'm hearing. "Why didn't you tell me this?"

"Because I knew I didn't stand a chance in court. And I didn't want to draw it out."

Fuck. "Max. We'll get you out of this, I promise."

I've always promised him the world. Sometimes I'm

not able to deliver, though, as hard as I might try. We both know that. We talk about it for a while and we discuss how to handle it. After he ends the call, I contact an investigator I use who's good and very discrete.

It's typical of Max. He'd rather take the fall than make the company look dirty. Even if he's innocent.

When he meets us at the entrance of the restaurant, his bracelet looks like a space age metal watch with red blinking lights on it. I don't want to talk about his case in front of Tess, who doesn't come across as a person who's likely to keep details like that from spreading like wildfire.

He's subdued. But since there's nothing more we can do about it tonight, we decide to celebrate. He's not in jail, first of all. Second, I'm getting married in two days. I only wish I could speed up time.

We walk into the small restaurant that Lexi's been wanting to try. It's been written up in the Times and she follows their social media links. She's finally getting into some of the apps and social media sites most people her age have been obsessed with for years by this point. Her old phone was so outdated and she'd been so focused on her studies, she never had time for things like Instagram. Now, she shows me a picture on her phone from the restaurant's account. It's a photograph of an apple pie. The caption says: *L.A. Times calls our pies The Best in Los Angeles, hands down!!*

Apple pie just so happens to be Max's favorite food.

I hope the place is good. There aren't that many restaurants in his zone. It's mainly retail and offices with a couple of fast food places. With any luck, this can become his new hang-out.

Lexi arranged for Tess to meet us so they can talk about some of the details of the wedding. Tess is doing Lexi's make-up and they have things to discuss.

Tess arrives as we're entering the restaurant. She rushes up to Lexi and hugs her in that over-excitable way she has.

Then she glances at Max. She moves toward him, maybe to give him a hug, but he barely flinches and takes a subtle step back. He doesn't like other people touching him. But he seems to have lost a degree of that quiet dread that hung to him earlier in the day. Nothing like dodging a ten-year sentence in a maximum-security prison to lighten a person's mood. "Thanks for venturing into my jurisdiction," he says, winking at Tess.

"For you?" she laughs, going a deep shade of pink. "Anything."

It's easy enough to read the dynamic. She's flirting with him like there's no tomorrow. Which is nothing unusual. Women throw themselves at Max all the time, and always have. He's tall, dark and mysterious with a twist: there's a hint of renegade angel in him, edged with the sincerity of a white knight. Tess is practically drooling.

Max, on the other hand, looks bored. I sincerely hope

he doesn't go for the easy lay, which is clearly on offer. I don't want Lexi to have any emotional melodramas to deal with on her wedding day. I know for a fact that Max would never stick with a girl like Tess beyond one night. She'd drive him insane before he'd even vacated her bed. This is as obvious as...well, pie.

Luckily Lexi seems to pick up on the vibe. She steers Tess's attention to some pictures on her phone as they slide deeper into the booth.

Max and I take a seat across from each other and the hostess offers us menus.

I start looking through the wine list. "What do you want?" I ask Max. He doesn't answer and when I look up at him, he's gazing at the hostess.

She has wavy strawberry-blond hair that's been tied up and pinned into place with a pencil—which isn't quite working. Strands have escaped to frame her face in loose ringlets. Her skin is pale and lightly freckled across her nose and the tops of her cheeks. She has bright blue eyes. She's slim but curvy, I can't help but notice—since Max is staring in a way that's, to be honest, sort of rude. She notices, and light flags of pink color her cheeks. She's stunningly pretty. She has the faintest ring of a bruise around one of her eyes that has faded almost completely, but not quite.

"Hi, and welcome to Peach's," she says, with a pronounced Southern drawl. "Your waitress will be with you in just a minute with our specials list for this evening. Can I get ya'll started with a drink from the bar?"

Max is still staring.

I decide to break his trance by ordering a drink. "We'll have a bottle of Krug. 1998 if you have it. I'll have a Jack Daniel's on ice and…Max?"

Max appears to be speechless. "What's your name?" he finally says.

"Peach." She smiles.

"Peach," he repeats. He's taken off his jacket and his sleeves are rolled up, revealing both the metal bracelet and several of his tattoos. "And this restaurant is called Peach's."

"It's my restaurant."

"You're a chef?" Max asks.

"And a baker, a hostess, sometimes a bartender. I sort of do it all."

"A baker," Max muses dreamily, like the occupation is the most erotic-sounding thing he's ever heard.

"Best apple pie in Los Angeles, according to the Times," I point out.

"No shit," he says, wildly impressed. He looks up at Peach. "Do you bake the apple pies?"

"Sure do." She's clearly proud of this.

"What kind of name is Peach?" Max presses. "Is that your real name?"

"Nope. My real name is Dixie Mae Rafferty Sutton. But

most people have been calling me Peach since I was about five. Ever since I baked my first pie, actually. It was a peach pie, in case you're wondering."

"Can't get more Southern than that," I comment, but neither of them are listening.

Max is riveted. He's acting like the information she's just given him is the most fascinating thing he's ever heard. "I *was* wondering, as a matter of fact." He's so quietly overblown about it, I almost wonder if he's joking. But when he asks his next question, his tone is anything but joking. "What happened to your eye?"

It isn't even appropriate, to ask something like that to a total stranger, but Max has a way about him that can get away with that kind of thing. The girl doesn't look pissed off about it. Instead of going pink, this time she pales a shade, and her hand ghosts to her cheek, where the bruise is barely visible. Her stricken expression is replaced by a smile so practiced, I think we both see it then: a habit we recognize. "Oh, that?" she says. "I walked into a door. Rushing around as much as I do, it happens."

Isn't that code for "someone hits me"? Maybe I'm just being paranoid, given my—Max's, more specifically— history. Then again, maybe when running a restaurant, with all that running in and out of doors, well, maybe you *do* occasionally bump into one.

Max has gone quiet, contemplating the girl.

"So," she says to him, sort of softly sassy about it, "Have you decided what you want yet?"

"As a matter of fact I have decided." He says this while looking directly into her eyes and her blush returns. It's several seconds before he continues. "I'll also have a Jack Daniel's on ice. And to start, I want a double slice of your apple pie, served warm with vanilla ice cream on the side."

Peach smiles at him, as though he's just given her the biggest compliment in the world by ordering a slice of her pie. She doesn't even question the fact that he's ordered dessert for an appetizer. "I *always* serve it warm with vanilla ice cream on the side. *Homemade* vanilla ice cream."

I can't help but laugh at the expression on Max's face as he watches her walk away. My concern about the possibility of Max having a one night stand with Tess is suddenly gone.

I have a feeling that Max is going to be frequenting Peach's on a very regular basis. Even more so when his homemade pie is delivered—which he eats like he's having some kind of orgasmic experience.

And I'm *exceptionally* relieved that Peach's is in his zone.

16

LEXI

"You and Tess are booked into a day spa, then the limo will take you to the house in Malibu, where a five course meal for fourteen—that's the number Tess gave me—will be served at seven o'clock. It's easier for you to sleep there, since the dress will arrive in the morning and all the people who will help you get ready need you there. The staff will help you with anything, just ask. And I'll be waiting for you at the altar at one pm and not a second later." My husband-to-be is nothing if not thorough.

"Where are you going to stay?"

"At Max's."

"You could stay in Malibu, too."

Rafe kisses me, for the millionth time. "I can't see you before the wedding. That would be bad luck. And I'm not taking any chances."

"I wouldn't have picked you for the superstitious type."

"Usually, I'm not. But I'm not willing to risk it either way."

"I love you."

"Love you more, baby girl. And I hate leaving you. The next time I see you we'll be taking our vows. I can't wait." He kisses me again, lingers, then heads toward the door. "Have fun tonight. But not *too* much fun." He blows me a kiss. And then he's gone.

God.

Who knew a person could get so ridiculously addicted to another person? It hurts, watching him walk away.

The day is surreal, for many reasons. Already, I miss him on an aching, profound level that seems to tug at the roots of my soul. I can't wait to see him at the altar in all his dark glory. I can't wait to get started.

Until then, the day is perfect. He might even have paid off the weather gods. The sky is as blue as I've ever seen it. I get into the limo that's waiting for me in front of Rafe's building. The city is colorful and vibrant as we drive toward Tess's.

Tess is buzzing.

Even though she struck out with Max last night, Tess is already (sort of) moving on. "I guess he's not really my type," she's rambling. "I mean, it's all fine to go for the bad boy, but he'd be so moody! Who wants to deal with that all the time? Anyway, we'll see him tomorrow and now that I'm working at Downtown, I'm bound to run into him from time to time. Plus he'll be your new brother in law, so we can all hang out."

"Exactly," I agree, even though I'm relieved. I just have this feeling he'd steamroll her heart without even noticing. It's better this way.

The day spa has a view of the ocean. It's fabulous and totally over the top. We're served mimosas and platters of fruit, caviar, chocolate and warm, buttery croissants.

We're sitting in a hot tub, sipping our drinks, and Tess burst out laughing. "Holy fuck, Lexi. You are the luckiest girl in the *world*. I mean, *look* at all this! Look at your *life*."

"I know." It's true. *Can perfection last?* is what I'm wondering. Is a life that seems too good to be true...well, *too good to be true*? I can admit to myself that there's something daunting about it all. I can savor every detail, but still, the heights are dizzying at times, when you realize the only way to go from here is down.

But I'm no pessimist. I laugh with her and clink my glass against hers. We spend the day getting massaged, groomed, styled and pampered in every way imaginable.

"So, whatever happened with the supermodel ex-girlfriend?" Tess asks. I'd told her about some of the details of my run-in with Vanessa.

"She's been calling. She wants to see Rafe, but he's refusing."

"I guess he's not the kind of guy you'd let go of without a fight."

"No," I agree.

"What else could she possibly have to say to him? She must be a total glutton for punishment."

"I've wondered the same thing. How many times does she need to be told no?"

"It's not like she even needs the money," Tess comments, and I'll admit, it riles me a little. Rafe's money is the least interesting thing about him.

After we're finished at the spa, the limo takes us to Rafe's Malibu estate.

Tess gasps as we drive through the gates. "Holy shit," she says weakly. The house is ultra-modern, with a huge, very-elaborate garden that slopes down the lawn, over-looking the ocean view, which is spectacular. The water is mirror-calm and bright blue. There's an infinity pool, topiaries and white sand trails that lead down to a small sandy bay with its own secluded beach.

Wow.

It's like a dream. Rafe's perfect world.

His staff are everywhere, busily preparing for the wedding. We're shown to Rafe's master bedroom, which looks like something straight out of a luxury seaside homes magazine spread. Double French doors are open to the view of the balcony and the ocean. We're fawned over, and served more champagne.

The wedding planner's name is Avery. Tess helps me with a few last minute details before we take a walk down to the beach. Later, we have dinner with the people Tess has invited, who are more her friends than mine, but it's fun and festive and they all toast to me, to Rafe, to a happy and long-lasting marriage.

I hope we're not rushing this. I hope we do get our happy ever after and that everything is as charmed as it seems.

In the morning, Tess does my make-up as a stylist does my hair. The dress arrives with its team and it's even more exquisite than I remember it.

"Oh, Lex. *Look* at you." Tess has tears in her eyes and so do I. "No. Oh god, I'm going to have to touch you up. Lex, you look so beautiful."

I glance at myself in the full-length mirror and it *is* like a dream.

I look like someone else.

Someone perfect.

Someone exquisite and wealthy and privileged and pink-cheeked from champagne and love and happiness. The fleeting uneasiness surfaces but quickly passes: there are so many imperfect layers to me, buried and damaged and simmering away unseen.

But Rafe knows about all that. He loves me anyway.

And I can't wait to see him. The urge feels unbearable. I feel the ache of this distance in my heart and in my throat. I really don't care about all these extras. I just want him.

"Are you ready?" It's Avery and her team, standing around me, handing me my bridal bouquet. White roses. They're so beautiful they don't look real. Just like everything else.

"I'm ready."

I float down the curved staircase. There are flowers everywhere, a sea of white roses and bouquets of pink peonies. Live music softly wafts through the gentle sea breeze.

Max offered to walk me down the aisle, since I don't have anyone else. He's standing at the bottom of the stairs and he's smiling at me. He crooks his arm for me and I hold onto him for support. "Wow," he says. "You look fucking gorgeous, Lex."

"Thanks." I feel shy and excited and nervous. I'm glad Max is here. He feels solid and warm and strong and his presence eases my nerves. He's ridiculously handsome in his tux. "You scrub up pretty good, too," I tell him.

He gives me a smile that's so full of compassion it almost brings tears to my eyes. But Tess would kill me if I mess up my make-up again. "You ready?" he says. "I can tell you, my brother has been *unbearable* all day. Chomping at the bit, you could say." Max's fitted bracelet glints in the sun. "What do you think of my new bling?"

"I think it adds character."

He laughs and takes my hand, fingering my diamond.

"And it cost even more than *your* new bling." That sardonic tough-guy drawl is pure Max.

I hear it then. The band has started playing the wedding march. Tess has the rings and the plan is for her to go first.

"Ready?" she whispers. She seems as nervous as I feel.

"Let's do this," Max says encouragingly.

Tess squeezes my hand. "I love you, Lex," she whispers, then she starts walking down the aisle.

Max leads me out of the roomy, marble-floored hall and out into the garden.

Guests are gathered there, the blue sea behind and the puffed pink and white of a thousand flowers. I barely notice any of it.

There he is.

Strapping and dark and sexy as hell in his black tux. Without a doubt, the most beautiful sight in this world.

As we walk closer I can see it mirrored in his eyes. Amazement, love, a careful, contained happiness. His eyes never leave me. His concentration is riveted, just like mine.

Tess takes her place to the left of the altar. And Max raises my veil and kisses my cheek, then he places my hand in Rafe's.

Rafe looks starstruck. He leans to whisper in my ear. "Angel, you are *stunning.*"

"So are you."

We take our places at the altar and the celebrant

begins to speak. "Ladies and gentlemen, we are gathered here today to—"

A commotion causes the celebrant to pause and look up.

People are murmuring. They're moving...to allow someone through.

Someone who is irate and loud and storming her way to the front of the crowd.

Oh no.

No.

Please, no.

Vanessa.

She rushes up to us, windblown and red-faced and undone-looking, like she's on the verge of some sort of breakdown.

"Stop!" she says, her palms raised. "Rafe!"

The shrill sound of her voice pops the bubble of this perfect day and this perfect place. The band stops playing.

Everything goes quiet, except for her.

"You don't answer my calls and now I find out your getting married *today*? Why didn't you tell me?"

People are attempting to guide Vanessa away. But it's too late to restore anything resembling peace, and Vanessa shrugs them off violently. "Get off me!" she shrieks.

Rafe looks stunned. Max steps forward. "Vanessa... what the fuck? You have no business—"

Vanessa cuts him off, speaking only to Rafe. "If you'd

just bothered to *meet* with me, after I *told* you a thousand times I have something I wanted to tell you in person. *Privately*. But now it's too late for that."

The next three words shatter everything. They break the pure beauty of this day. They bring everything to a screeching, heart-breaking halt.

"Rafe," Vanessa says. "I'm pregnant."

17

———

RAFE

No. No no no no no no no no no no no no no no no no. *No.*

"You can't be." This can't be happening.

"I *am!*" Vanessa cries. "And don't even ask me if it's yours! You're the only person I've been with in the last year. It must have happened that night."

Fuck. *Fuck.* I know what night she's talking about. A nightmare of a night. The night the condom broke. I was furious, and she was furious about how furious I was. It shouldn't have broken. Condoms don't just randomly *break*. The thought had crossed my mind then: she sabotaged me. It was more than a hunch. I *knew* she was capable of doing something like that. I knew how badly she wanted to keep things the way they were. Her desperation was the biggest thing about her. *It wouldn't be the end of the world*, she'd said. *We were thinking of getting married anyway.*

No.

I made the decision that night. I was done.

I'd forgotten about it. Put it out of my mind. I'd been preoccupied with Max and work and, most of all, Lexi. Always Lexi.

It feels like years ago now, but it wasn't. A month or two, at the most. Just a short time before Lexi stormed into my life and changed everything.

And now this. Now a lifetime of being tied to Vanessa.

I know she'll want to keep it and I wouldn't ask her not to. In a deep corner of my psyche that I can in no way analyze at this particular moment, I don't think terminating a life is the right thing to do, but I also firmly believe it should be a woman's choice. Vanessa would never make that choice. Not after scheming to make it happen in the first place.

Is she lying? Also something she's capable of. But, Jesus, would she take it this far? Would she lie about something this sacred just to ruin our day?

In this moment, I don't care about any of that. All I care about is trying like hell to hold on to—*I can feel it*—what is starting to slip through my fingers.

Lexi.

There, behind her tear-filled green eyes, I see it. A shift.

Please. Please, no.

"Lexi," I plead. I *know* what she's thinking. I know how she'll be reacting to this news. It's the one thing that could take her from me. The *one thing* she'll never be able to overlook. "It doesn't matter," I tell her. "We can deal with this."

"It doesn't *matter*? Of course it matters. That baby needs you."

It hits me hard, the way she says that. On a million different levels. There's so much at play here my head is spinning.

Lexi gathers her feather skirt and turns away from me, as though to run. I reach for her arm but she pulls away.

She gives me a look that's so haunted and so pleading I feel it all the way to the bottom of my soul. "Rafe," she says, her face streaked now with make-up. "Babies need their fathers. Babies whose fathers walk out on them have terrible, unhappy lives, I know that only too well and so do you. I can't do that to someone else. And I can't let *you* do that. I don't want you to follow me. I don't want you to track me or have your investigators keep tabs on me. I need to think this through, in my own way and in my own time. If there's anything left of me when I figure that out, I'll let you know. If you care about me at all, don't try to stop me. Give me some time. Listen to what I'm asking you now: let me go. Please, just *let me go*."

She leaves me standing there as she walks away.

18

I RUN UP THE STAIRS. I hear people calling after me but I don't look back. I grab the small suitcase I brought for the weekend, then I take the stairs that lead down from the balcony of the master bedroom, finding my way to the back of the house. I don't want to see Max or even Tess. I need to be alone, where I can retreat back into myself and find my own way. It's the only way I can cope with this.

The loss is astoundingly heavy.

I don't want to talk about it or cry about it or share it. I just want to own it and let it overtake me. I want to disappear, like I'm so good at doing.

I make my way along a path through a side garden that's bursting with blue and pink flowers. A colorful, awful reminder. Will it be a perfect blue-eyed boy? Or a beautiful, dark-haired baby girl?

Several limos are parked on the driveway. I recognize

one of the drivers, who's leaning against his limo scrolling on his phone.

I walk over to him and he watches me approach. "Could you give me a ride?"

He looks at my dress questioningly, but doesn't ask. It's probably pretty obvious—by my dress, the state of my make-up, the fact that there's no groom to be seen—that something has gone terribly wrong. "You got it, honey." He opens the door for me.

I have my bag this time. My phone, a change of clothes. And my money cards. I'll use them. Rafe would want me to, I know that. Just until I get on my feet. Then I'll cut them up and leave him to his new life with his new baby. Maybe he and Vanessa can work through their differences. They're similar people, after all. Super successful. Rich. Driven. Maybe they can make it work for the sake of their child.

As if I'm going to let Rafe walk out on his own baby, just like my father so irrevocably did to me. Even the fact that Rafe was *willing* to do that...maybe he's not the man I thought he was.

I don't know.

I can't think. I feel disoriented by my sorrow.

"Where to, miss?" the driver asks.

"Please take me to LAX."

He tips his hat through the rear-view mirror and we start driving.

Where should I go?

Home? Never. A team of wild horses couldn't drag me back to Oregon.

Venice? I've always wanted to see that place. It's hard to imagine a city whose roads are canals. I've never been out of the United States. Where would he have taken me for our honeymoon? He said he was going to surprise me. I told him anywhere but Paris. That was what *she* had wanted. He'd agreed. Not Paris, even though he wanted to take me there later, he said. He was going to save Paris for our six-month anniversary.

Maybe she'll get that Parisian honeymoon now, after all.

I could go to New York. It's far away from here. No one will know me. I can disappear. Find a job. Get an apartment. It would be a good place to start over.

As good a place as any.

I don't want to stay in California. I might bump into... them. Their little family unit. Their baby, who promises to be as perfect as a baby can be.

I force myself to cope. I have a plan now. I'm going to New York because I can't think further than getting on a place and I need a destination. Now all I need to do is put one foot in front of the other.

The limo ride takes an hour or so. My thoughts are hazy, replaying the pain and the beauty in equal measure. I don't know what to think about. All I know is that I need to get away from him. I need to give him space to figure out, with the mother of his child, what he's going to do. That baby needs his undivided attention, which it'll never get if I'm in the way.

I thank the driver. I try to pay him, but he waves my card away. "Mr. Black will take care of it, I'm sure." Of course he will.

I walk into the airport, finding the booking desk. People are staring. I'm still in my wedding dress. I try to wipe my smeared make-up with my fingers. I use the card Rafe gave me to pay for the ticket. *They're yours, to use however you want. Both accounts are in your name and have five hundred thousand dollars loaded, but we can top them up if you need more.*

While I'm waiting to board the flight, I go into the bathroom. I take off my wedding dress and roll it up. I can't bring myself to throw it away so I stuff it carefully into my bag. I put on the outfit I was going to wear the next day. To travel in. To wherever he was going to take me. It's a six thousand dollar black jumpsuit Rafe bought for me that day on Rodeo Drive. It was the only piece of clothing that had a price tag still attached, which the shop assistant must have forgotten to remove. *Six thousand dollars,* I'd marveled at the time. Since then, I'd almost become accustomed to the luxury and the no-expense-spared lifestyle.

I wipe off all my make-up and smooth my hair. I stare at myself in the bathroom mirror.

Here's the real me. The one who's used to struggling and being alone.

What was I thinking, pretending I was destined for something more?

The boarding call is announced and I get in line. I take my phone out of my bag and text Tess, who's already left me 17 messages. *Don't worry about me. I need some time. I'll be okay. Tell Max. And tell Rafe: he needs to do the right thing. He knows that. I love you, Tess. Be good xx*

Then I turn off my phone and board the plane.

We take off and I look down over the vast sprawl of L.A., all the way to the coastline.

The sun hangs low over the water, painting the ocean brilliant shades of orange and red.

It'll be a beautiful sunset tonight in Malibu.

19

———

RAFE

I FALL to my knees as she walks away.

I hear Max call after her, but she doesn't turn.

Her words pound through my brain in repeating echoes. *If you care about me at all, don't try to stop me. Give me some time. Let me go. Please, just let me go.*

Words that dig into my heart like jagged, spearing knives.

How can she ask this of me?

How can she leave me?

That look in her eyes, so soulful and wounded. If I follow her, if I refuse to respect her request, she might never take me back.

Let me go.

My golden girl. My angel. Everything I've ever wanted out of life, delivered to me in one perfect package.

Gone.

I'm vaguely aware that the wedding planner has already cleared the crowd, ushering them into the house. The band is packing up.

Max pulls me to my feet.

It's only Max and Vanessa standing there. Max's hand is on my shoulder. Vanessa reaches for me. To touch my hand.

I jerk away before she can make contact. Something fierce and dangerous rages inside me. I almost fear for her safety. *She just destroyed my fucking life.* But then I remember: the baby.

"Rafe," she says softly. No longer shrill. She got her way. She won. She's patient and caring now.

I look into her eyes and all I can feel for her is an almost alarming wave of hatred. She might see a degree of it, and tears begin to pool in her eyes. *Good. I want her to suffer.*

I'd once thought her beautiful, in a severe sort of way. Now all I can see is the horrible, calculating ugliness that has stolen the one true thing in my life. Vanessa may or may not have intentionally tampered with the condom that night. She may or may not be lying about her pregnancy. She's upset now, at my indifference, but there's that spark of glee in there, too. Her plan worked.

When I start speaking, my voice sounds strange. Hard and cold and dead. Something in me has been irrevocably broken. "You'll get the best healthcare money can provide. For the baby's sake. We can fight out the custody arrangement when the time comes. But let me be crystal clear: I do not want to see you or hear from you until the baby is born. The only reason I will ever see you again is to do the right thing for my child. If it even *is* my child, which will be determined incontestably with a DNA test as soon as it's safe to do so. You and I are over. There is no relationship between us. Now or ever."

Tears stream down her cheeks. I feel nothing.

"Get out of my house."

"But, Rafe—"

"*Get out.*"

It's a good thing Max guides her away because I'm on the brink of losing something. My sanity, maybe. He gets some people to take Vanessa out. They comfort her as she sobs.

Who's comforting Lexi?

Where will she go?

I can't handle this.

"Max, get me a drink."

He contemplates me for a second. He does what I ask and thank fuck he's not going to try to give me a lecture or a pep talk. He comes back with a bottle of Jack and he slings his arm around me and leads me down the sandy path that winds down to the beach. The beach has been set up with a gauzy marquee with glass chandeliers. There are blankets and ottomans and flowers and champagne buckets on ice. No one's here.

We sit on the sand at the other end of the beach from the marquee. The sun is starting to set. I take a long drink from the bottle.

We pass it back and forth for a while.

"She'll come back," Max says. "She just needs a little time."

Will she?

What if she doesn't?

Will I survive this?

20

NEW YORK CITY IS CROWDED. It's raining and cold.

Why didn't I go somewhere warm? It was a resolution of mine somewhere along the way. Avoiding cold places. But there's an energy here I might have almost been able to appreciate if circumstances were different.

I walk along the streets with my small bag, completely directionless.

I remember Rafe saying he has a place here. I wonder where it is.

God, we would have had fun exploring these streets together. The city would have looked different with him in it, like everything did. Infused with that gold dust he seemed to sprinkle over everything, making colors brighter. Sparking the world with excitement and hope.

Without him, the world looks gray. Bleak and dismal.

New York is made for walking, compared to L.A.'s

sprawl. It's tall and stoic and old-feeling. Walking through its streets doesn't feel dangerous. There are landmarks I recognize from movies and T.V. shows. The Empire State Building. Central Park. Rockefeller Center. I stand and watch the people ice skating for a while. Holding hands. Laughing with their children.

I wish I could tell him I'm sorry for leaving him.

That I simply can't live with the knowledge that—just by being together—we've stolen that baby's family. I know what abandonment feels like. It's the single worst thing that's ever happened to me. I just couldn't live with that.

I hope he remembers the things I told him.

I hope he knows.

21

RAFE

THE NIGHT BECOMES A BLURRY, soft stupor. The agony is there, hanging out at the fringes. But here, inside my shelter of inebriation, it's okay. I can still breathe. My heart is still beating, even if it has lost its rhythm, skipping beats because it's broken.

That's what she's taken with her. Those beats of my heart that just don't happen sometimes.

"Max?"

"Over here."

We're still on the beach. I'm lying here in my tux and it's covered in sand. And wet. My shirt is open. My tie is long gone. I'm barefoot. "Did we go swimming?"

"You wanted to. But I pulled you back."

"You should've just let me fucking float away." It would have been peaceful out there.

"Nope." He's sitting up, a few feet away.

"You should have," I say.

"What would I tell Lexi when she comes back?"

"She's not coming back. She told me she wasn't."

"She didn't say she's never coming back. She just said she needed some time."

"I'm going after her."

"You can't, Rafe. She asked you not to. Just give her a little time."

"No. I'm going after her like a caveman and bringing her back."

"Rafe," Max says patiently. "She asked you not to do that."

"I don't care." I'm holding the bottle of whiskey. I take another swig. It's practically fucking empty. "Who drank all this?"

Max just smiles, but it's a sad smile. "You, mostly. Me, some."

I sit up a little. The whole world tilts and swirls for a few seconds. I look out at what Max is looking at, the glimmer of the moonlight on the waves. "Why are there two moons?"

"Because you're fucking wasted, that's why."

"She did it on purpose, you know."

"Who did what on purpose?" Max is drawing pictures in the sand with a piece of driftwood.

"Vanessa. Since when do condoms just randomly get holes in 'em? That's what I want to know."

"Not often."

"Exactly." I try to focus, but can't. Those moons are fucking *beautiful*. Fuck. "It really would've been a nice night to be married."

"She'll come around, Rafe. You'll see."

"God, Max. I just fucking fell in *love*, from that very first moment. How does that even happen? I wasn't expecting it at all." I'm ranting, but I don't care. "There I was, just minding my own business—I was actually *regretting* that I'd agreed to interview the last candidate because it was my birthday and it was a Friday afternoon, can you believe that? And then in she walks and—*boom*, that was *it*. It was like taking a direct hit in the chest from a million-watt lightning bolt." It still hurts. I can still feel it. "Can you die from loving someone too much?"

"I don't know, Rafe."

"*Now* what the fuck am I supposed to do? She's *gone*. I don't know if I can take it, Max, I really don't. I don't *want* to live without her! I don't. What's the fucking point of *that*?" Max is right. I'm wasted.

"She'll come back."

"What if she doesn't? Then what?"

"Then you'll get on with your life."

"I don't want to get on with my life without Lexi in it."

"You have to. You have to skim along the surface of each day and ignore all the absences and memories and just pretend like they don't exist. Some days it'll be more than you can bear. Sometimes you'll feel like you've lost your mind. Some nights you'll feel like it isn't worth it. But it is. Because there will be other days when you remember what the good stuff feels like. That day Lexi comes back to you, you'll think: See? This was worth it. So you just have to wait it out and let her make her own decision, without forcing her hand. That's what you have to do."

"It is?"

"Yeah. It is."

"Fuck." God, I'm tired. "I don't want to do that. I'm going after her, Max."

"Remember how she asked you not to do that, Rafe? I think you should listen."

"She doesn't understand. I need her."

"I think you should give her a little time."

"You do?"

"Yeah."

"What if it kills me?"

"It won't."

"*It will.*"

"You could take some time off, you know, Rafe. I could find someone to run things for a while. If you wanted. Go to Hawaii. Just chill and get your head together."

My chest feels unbearably heavy. "Hawaii won't get my head together. It'll remind me of her."

"Yeah. I guess it will."

I laugh morosely. "I actually had to pinch myself sometimes. I'd wake up with her next to me and I'd literally pinch myself because I thought I was dreaming."

"I can see why you would've done that," he says.

"I don't want to live without her."

"You have to."

"What if I can't?"

"You can."

We're quiet for a while. Two identical wispy clouds drift across the moons.

"You know," Max says. "It might be a good idea to get Vanessa to take a court-ordered pregnancy test by one of your own doctors. Just in case she's lying."

"Yeah." My voice sounds exhausted, defeated.

"I'll take care of it if you want."

I'm glad he's offering that. Because I don't feel capable of doing anything. I have serious doubts I'll even be able to drag myself off this beach before high tide. Max will have to do that for me, too. I almost wish he'd go away, so I could float out to sea and be free. I don't want to deal with anyone or try so damn hard anymore. I feel like my trying-hard mechanism has broken, along with my heart.

"Come on." Max stands up and holds a hand out to me. "We'll get some sleep, then head back to the city. I have to be back by eight. Or it's off to jail, where they'll lock me up for three years and throw away the key."

This reminds me of Lexi. The key.

I hope she's okay.

I hope she's not cold. I hope she uses the money and checks herself into a nice hotel somewhere and gets room service. I hope she's safe.

Please come back to me, baby.

Please, please come back.

22

———

RAFE

"I'm not going back to the city," I tell Max. "You can drop me off at the marina." It's safe to say I have never felt worse in the entirety of my life. The pummeling hangover is the least of it. I'm drained. Gone. Dead, for all intents and purposes. I can't find who I used to be. I couldn't have laughed or cried at gunpoint.

"Are you sure that's a good idea?" Max says.

I have a 40-foot sailboat I take out from time to time. "Yes. You can hold down the fort for me. I need to disappear for a while."

He's watching me. Sailing is something we used to do with our father, all those years ago. Before he went bankrupt and shot himself. A long time ago, I can vaguely remember him differently. Young and handsome and carefree.

It's one of the reasons I've worked so hard. So I

wouldn't repeat his mistakes. In a way, I'd wanted to fix my father's problems, by following in his footsteps, by getting it right where he'd fucked up. It's stupid, really. He's been gone for a long time.

"I don't want you disappearing on me, Rafe."

"Just for a while." I don't need to explain. He gets it. "I need a break."

If anyone is going to understand that sentiment, it'll be Max. I haven't had a break from my responsibilities, well, ever. Not since Max was a tiny little kid. I never *wanted* a break before. But without Lexi, what's the point? She's taken everything: my will, my drive, the fun, the beauty. All of it.

"I don't want to go back to that apartment without her in it." The office will be even worse.

"Where are you going to go?"

"South. Mexico, maybe."

"Rafe. Just come back with me. Please. Stay in my apartment for a while. I could use the company."

"I can't. I need some space. I need to think."

"You can think on dry land, Rafe. Don't take the boat out. You're not in the right mind to sail."

"I'm in exactly the right mind to sail. I'm going, Max. You can't stop me, so don't try to."

He's worried as hell, but unless he knocks me out or locks me up, there's not a damn thing he can do to keep me here. "I'd come with you if I could."

"I know."

"Keep in touch with me, Rafe. Answer your goddamn phone. I mean it, okay? I don't want to be calling the fucking Coast Guard."

"Sure."

"I'll call the lawyers and get that pregnancy test confirmed, one way or the other."

"Thanks."

"Rafe?"

We're pulling up at the marina. "Yeah?"

"Don't do anything stupid."

That's an assurance I simply can't give. "Call me if you hear from her."

"Of course I will." Max gives me a hug. "Take care of yourself, brother."

"You too, punk." I step out of the limo and walk over to my boat.

Within the hour, I'm heading out to sea.

Devastated.

Broken.

Alone.

23

I WAKE UP. I'm lying curled on a park bench. I used my bag as a pillow and—thankfully—it's still here.

The sun is already up and there are people, in the distance, milling around, exercising and so on, getting on with their lives.

It's weird how light I feel. How loose and adrift. But not scared. Rafe broke something open in me and allowed his light to begin to heal me. Now all the fear has somehow leaked out of that same fissure. Even now, I can feel the strength he gave me.

I wonder how he is.

Has he worked things through with Vanessa? Have they come up with a plan about how they'll raise their child? The heartache is all-encompassing, almost staggeringly so. But I know it was the right thing to do, to give their baby a chance at a family. Just a chance. I couldn't live with myself if I stood in the way of all that. Like a roadblock to that little child's perfect world.

Has he gone back to work? He might be back in his office by now, making phone calls, answering emails. Uninterrupted.

My stomach growls and I realize I haven't eaten anything in almost twenty-four hours. Breakfast, with Tess. At the spa.

I decide I'll stay in a hotel for a few days and look for a job. I'll use Rafe's money until I can make enough to fend for myself. I know he'd want me to. But I'm not going to use more than I need to. I have a degree, after all. It was only three weeks ago that I...interviewed for the job at Downtown. There's no reason I can't get something equally as good—okay, not *equally*, in any regard—but good enough, here in New York.

But first I need to eat something. I walk along for a while until I find a restaurant. It's all light wood inside with big windows. Inside, it's warm and inviting.

I sit at a small table next to a window.

A waiter comes almost immediately. He's young, probably close to my age or a few years older. He's tall and all-American-looking with brown hair, squared shoulders and a clean-cut vibe. One of those guys that was probably a lacrosse star in high school. He has that grounded, happy-go-lucky aura to him, the kind you can only get by growing up in a big, character-laden house with basements and turrets and gardens, surrounded by a mother who cooks and a strapping father and lots of siblings: maybe a bookish one and a quirky one and a brooding older sister whose friends all have the hots for Joe Lacrosse over here. He's the type of guy you could write a hometown romance novel about. Maybe set in Cape Cod, or Vermont. Or maybe not; I might just be dazed from lack of sleep.

He's staring at me, as though shell-shocked by something. Maybe I remind him of someone. "Hi, I'm Ollie. I'll be your server."

"Hi, Ollie. I'm Lexi." I don't know why I tell him my name. Probably because he told me his. It seems polite.

"Hi, Lexi. Nice to meet you." A light heat rises to his cheeks. His embarrassment, at something so tame, is not quite what I'm used to. He smiles and it's a smile so open and baggage-free I can't help but stare.

"What can I get you?" he says.

"An iced tea. And an omelet."

Ollie studies me for a few seconds, his eyes taking in the slightly-disheveled state of me. My hand involuntarily touches my hair. I haven't even looked in the mirror since I got off the plane.

He hands me a glass of water from the tray he's carrying and as I reach for it, his fingers graze mine. This causes another open, barely-bashful smile to light up his face. He's handsome, I realize. It's a fresh, youthful handsomeness. I'm so used to the seasoned all-out masculinity of Rafe, but as I consider this stranger more carefully, I can see it, that super-upright build, that sunny demeanor. I'm sure he broke a few hearts back in Vermont.

"Wow," he says.

"Wow?"

"Sorry. It's just...your eyes are very green." He smiles again. "I'm sorry. What kind of omelet do you want?"

God, why did I order an omelet, of all things? I think of Rafe, cooking me breakfast in Hawaii. *In his board shorts and nothing else. Burning his finger on the toast. His blue eyes. Taking such care with me as he taught me to surf.* I wait for that all-too-familiar sting of tears, but it doesn't come. I'm all cried out. I'm numb. I have to move on, and get on with my life, for reasons I've already agonized over too many times to count. "Um, a cheese omelet, please."

"I'll put the order in and then, well, my shift actually finishes in about ten minutes. Could I...I mean...would you want to have breakfast...with me? Only if you don't mind."

I don't mind. Sure. I say the things that sound like they should be said.

But it's worrying me how I feel nothing.

Just...nothing.

It's just an empty space where feeling used to live.

I watch Ollie walk away to place my order and all I can

feel is a sort of unhinged madness sitting next to me, like a shadow.

Am I losing my mind?

Everything about me feels completely, unfathomably empty.

24

RAFE

I RUMMAGE through the supplies below deck, finding what I'm looking for. I have a guy who keeps it stocked, in case I want to take people out. Work colleagues, people I need to impress for one reason or another.

I'm still wearing my tux. It's damp and wrinkled. Covered in sand. I take it off and find a pair of old cotton shorts.

I take the bottle up on deck, not particularly worried about my new habit of drinking copious amounts of alcohol for one reason and one reason only. To forget.

Sitting back onto the low, cushioned seat, I vaguely appreciate the scene. The sun. Waves.

I pour a generous amount of red wine into a glass. All the way to the brim. It looks like blood.

Not a great idea, of course, getting inebriated while at sea.

Today, though, it makes perfect sense. It fits what I need from this day.

Recklessness.

Open water.

Isolation.

I sit there looking out at the sea and the sky. I don't allow myself to think about anything at all, except the curl of the waves and the swarm of sharks that might possibly be circling somewhere below me. The wine is helping. I pour myself another glass.

Until I've drunk the whole bottle.

Then I open another one.

25

I EAT BREAKFAST WITH OLLIE, and he talks the whole time. Turns out he isn't a lacrosse player, but captain of the swim team. He *did* grow up in a rambling house with his parents and siblings, not in Vermont but somewhere in New Hampshire. I *could* write a novel about it, with all the talking he does, which is fine.

I have nothing to say. I sit here and listen, so weary with heartache I feel almost dizzy.

"Lexi?"

"Yes?"

"Are you all right? Would you like to go home now?"

Home.

Damn. *Yes, I would, Ollie. I would like to go home. To him. He's my home. I miss him so much I think I might be losing my grip.*

I realize he's waiting for my answer. "Where do you live? I'll walk you there."

"I, uh, I actually just moved here. I haven't found a place yet. I'm staying in a hotel until I find something. Do you know of any good ones nearby?"

"You don't know where you're staying?"

"Not yet."

"Lexi?"

I realize I'm acting strange. Unusual. I make an effort to seem more relaxed. I smile at him. "Sorry. I think I'm a little jet-lagged. It was nice to meet you, Ollie. I'll go now."

He's staring at me in that layered way again. "Do you want...I have a studio apartment that's right around the corner. You're...I mean, you could stay there if you want. With me."

"What?"

"It's no trouble at all."

He has hazel eyes, almost amber-colored. "No. I'm just going to find a hotel."

"It's really not a big deal for you to crash at my place for a night or two. I promise, I don't bite. It'll give you a chance to look around."

My instincts are pretty good at detecting danger and I sense immediately that Ollie is about as unthreatening as a person can be. His mother taught him good manners, and he's making a genuine offer. Still. It's a terrible idea. "It's fine, really. Thank you, but—"

"I only moved to New York myself around a month ago. My sister was supposed to come with me but she met someone. It'd be nice to have the company. And it's clean, I promise."

Someone like Ollie would be a much better fit for me, really. I know what he's doing. It's unthreatening, it's genuine. There'd be no volatility or drama. I can see how a life with someone like this would play out. It would be as easy as following him now, to his clean little apartment that's probably decorated with candles and photos of his family. There's an old record player in the corner where he keeps his dad's vinyl collection, or something. We'd never argue. The sex would be tame and respectful. All good things.

All things that belong to someone else.

I'm too jagged.

I want Rafe's rough edges. I *crave* them. They fit me perfectly. I love his crazy passion and his stormy eyes. I've given all that up, but I can't...replace it with something less. I'll never recover from Rafe. Nothing will ever be as beautiful or forceful or as...*mine*. He was imperfectly perfect. He was the one.

"Thank you. But no. I've got to go now. I'm meeting someone," I lie, just to make this easier. "You take care, Ollie."

"Sure." He can hear that my decision is final, maybe. He doesn't protest. He's disappointed, but hell, aren't we all. "Breakfast is one me."

"Thanks." I walk away.

I spend the entire day walking. I walk Fifth Avenue, until I find a hotel with a big, open entrance and lots of lights. It looks like the kind of place Rafe would stay in.

For him, I go in and book myself a room. It's nice, with a huge bed and plush furnishings.

I turn my phone on and plug it in. There are 34 messages from Tess.

None from Rafe.

Good. I told him not to, and he's listening.

I listen to a few of Tess's messages and decide to call her. She answers on the first ring.

"Lexi? Jesus Christ, I've been so worried. Where are you?"

"I told you not to worry."

"Are you okay? Where are you?" she asks again.

I exhale a breath, like a hollow laugh. "Guess."

"What? I can't guess. Are you in L.A.? Let me come get you."

"I'm in New York."

"What? Why?"

"I felt like getting out of L.A."

"I can understand that, but...*New York*? Where are you staying?"

"In a swanky hotel."

"Good girl. Max called me. Like, ten times. He got my

number from Olivia. He wanted to know if I'd heard from you. He's so worried, Lex."

"Where's...?" I can't even ask the question.

"He was still with Max. Max was taking care of him. He wasn't in great shape."

I'm sorry, Rafe. You'll be okay. You'll get over me.

"Lex?"

"Yeah?"

"Will you call Max? Or can I? At least let me tell him I've heard from you. And that you're okay."

"Sure. Can you call him?" I don't feel like calling Max right now. There's nothing to say that will fix this.

"Okay. I will. I'll let him know. Are you...do you want me to get a flight to New York? We could hang out. It could be fun."

"No. It's okay, Tess. I need to figure some things out for myself."

"Okay. I know. It's a shock. It's a nightmare. But it's not exactly his fault, Lex. I mean, it's partly his fault that it *happened*, but that was *before* he even met you."

"It doesn't matter, Tess."

She's quiet for a second. "I just think you're—"

"Please."

She sighs. "All right. We'll leave it for tonight. Call me tomorrow, though, okay? What time is it there? It must be late."

"It's midnight."

"Get some sleep and call me tomorrow."

"Sure."

We end the call and I take a long bath. Since I don't have anything else to wear, I wash my clothes and hang them to dry overnight. Then I crawl into the enormous bed.

And I drift into an uneasy sleep.

Someone's warm hand is holding mine.

Rafe.

He's here with me. I miss you, he says. I love you. I need you.

But someone else is here, too. Standing behind him.

It's her. With her dark eyes and her bee-stung lips. She's holding a small, wrapped...it's their baby...whose face...god, it looks like him.

Please, she's pleading. Let us have him. He's ours. We need him more.

I wake with a start.

My heart is beating fast.

Where am I?

I'm in a hotel room. I'm in New York.

It takes a long time for my heartbeat to slow.

It was just a nightmare. And one I need to accept.

We need him more.

26

———————

RAFE

I WAKE up on a hard surface.

The sun is hot.

Fuck. I'm on my goddamn boat.

My head feels like a bomb has already detonated in there and is thinking about doing it again.

I have no idea what time it is, what day it is or how long I've been...wherever I am. I've drifted. I can't see land.

I try to sit up, holding onto a metal bar for support. It will hurt to fall and crack my head on these fucking planks. Maybe I've already done it once or twice. Maybe that's why my head is so unbearably sore.

But I finally get myself into a sitting position, so that's something.

I reach into my pocket for my phone. It has one percent of battery life left. There are 324 emails and 57 messages. Are any from her? I scroll, searching.

No. Not a single one.

How does she expect me to do this? To bide my time while she makes up her mind? Sure, I can respect her wishes and all that fucking bullshit, but all it means is that we can't be together.

It'll kill me, that much I do know. I'm not geared up to sit back like this and just let her walk away. Without fighting. That's what she's done. She's stolen all my ammunition.

Fuck it.

I type my message and send it, before I can overthink it, which isn't likely at this point anyway.

I love you. I miss you. Where are you? Come back to me.

As soon as it's sent, my phone goes dead.

27

THE PING of my phone wakes me up.

I reach for it and check my messages.

I love you. I miss you. Where are you? Come back to me.

So much for crying myself out. The well of my tears, apparently, has refilled.

I do it anyway, even if I shouldn't. Even if it's going to make everything harder. Even if the letters are blurry.

I type my reply. I send it before I can second-guess myself. *I love you more.*

So will your baby, is the thought that echoes in my head and then of course I regret everything.

All those little cells dividing. You have to give credit where credit is due. It's impeccable DNA. A little super-model or quarterback is incubating, no doubt about it.

I think about what *our* baby would have looked like.

Would it have been blond and green-eyed, like me, or dark-haired and blue-eyed, like him? Or some magical little mixture.

I guess we'll never know.

I DECIDE to give myself one more day. Then I'll resume my job search and start looking for a place to live.

One more day, to do my best to crawl out from under this crushing heartbreak. I've never been a person who sits around having pity parties for myself but this one is beyond heavy. I've pieced myself back together before but it's harder to do when pieces are actually missing. When big chunks of you are just...gone. When you know for a fact you'll never quite be whole again.

I stare at his message, for the hundredth time.

I love you. I miss you. Where are you? Come back to me.

He hasn't replied. Which is good, probably. He's moving on, maybe. I have the urge to call him, to make sure he's okay.

God, how I want to do it.

It doesn't have to be this way, some subconscious voice whispers. *He's hurting, you know he is. It's there in his words. Talk to him. Listen to him. Let him tell you how he feels. Let him assure you, if that's what you need. Give him a chance to be the man your father never was.*

I can feel it happening by slow degrees. I'm crumbling.

Not crumbling, a little devil on my shoulder whispers. *You're getting stronger.* Or maybe it's the angel. *Where's your fighting spirit? Where's that girl who used to go after what she wanted against all odds? He can love you* and *his baby. It doesn't have to be one or the other.*

Maybe that's true. Just because my father flaked doesn't mean everyone will.

My phone pings.

PLEASE CALL ME LEXI. I NEED YOUR HELP ASAP.

It's from Max.

I press the call button. "Max?"

"*Fuck.* Lexi, Where the fuck *are* you?" Max sounds frantic. "Did you get my messages?"

"I...well, I haven't been—"

"He's gone."

"What do you mean 'gone'?"

"He took his boat out, the morning...after. I haven't heard from him since. His voice mail is full and he's not answering the SAT phone. I'm about to call the Coast Guard. He could be anywhere. He was in a terrible state of mind. I should never have let him go, but I couldn't stop him. I'm just praying he hasn't done anything stupid." Max falters.

No, that's not possible. *Is it?*

"Where are you?" Max says.

"I'm in New York."

"New York—? Jesus, Lexi! What the hell are you doing in New York?" Max's cool has clearly left the building and no wonder. "I need you *here*! You have to help me find him! I can't even leave my fucking apartment. How soon can you get to the airport? Lexi, he needs you. I mean it. For fuck's sake, please help me find him. Come back."

"All right, Max. All right." I've never heard Max sound so unhinged. It scares me more than anything could at this point. That he's *this* worried means something is seriously wrong. And it's all my fault. "I'll come now, Max. I'll get the next flight."

"Good. Go to his house in Malibu. Keep trying his number. Fuck, Lex, I know why you did what you did, okay? I don't blame you. But you got it wrong. You don't understand anything. You need to let him convince you of that. Do you love him?"

I'm not expecting the question. "Of course. I—"

"Then *tell* him that. Before he self-implodes. None of this is his fault, or yours. You two need to work it out, okay? Just come back and find him and let him prove himself to you. He will if you let him."

I'm crying again. Hell. "Okay. I know." That's the thing.

I know Rafe will. He's not my father. He's good. He's proven that to me over and over and, still, I left him.

"Lex. Our scars resurface in strange ways sometimes. It's not your fault. You had reason to do what you did, even if no one else understands it. Just—*please*—come back now."

"I will. I'll call you when I'm there, okay?"

"Good. Hurry. Let me know as soon as you've landed."

What have I done? Have I driven him to...something unthinkable?

I quickly get dressed and throw my phone into my bag. I go down to the front desk and pay my bill. "I need a taxi to the airport. I need to get there as fast as possible. It's an emergency."

The desk clerk is helpful. "We have a driver who can take you immediately."

On the way to the airport, I book the next flight to L.A. online. And I call Rafe.

As Max said, his phone goes straight to voice mail, and says his mailbox is full.

Why isn't he answering?

Seven hours later, I land at LAX. I call Max. There's still no word from Rafe. Max has called the Coast Guard and they're now searching for his boat.

The taxi drops me off at Rafe's Malibu house. The housekeeper lets me in and I tell her the staff can take the next few days off. She doesn't question this and within the hour I'm all alone in Rafe's mansion. I keep trying to call him. And I stare out at the ocean as I wait for news.

My phone rings and it's Max again. There's still no sign of Rafe. "We got the results of the pregnancy test back," he says. "Vanessa finally agreed to it. It was negative. She's not pregnant."

"*What?* My god, Max."

"Yeah. And Rafe doesn't know."

"I'll tell him. As soon as he gets back."

If he gets back.

"I'm sorry, Max."

"It's not your fault, honey. None of it is. We're all just trying like hell to do the right thing. Some days it's easier than others."

"Where could he be?"

"He knows his way around a boat. He'll be fine. He's probably passed out or something. As soon as he wakes up, I'm sure he'll sail his way home."

I'm too choked up to answer.

Max sounds choked up, too. "We'll keep in touch, okay?

After Max hangs up, I walk down to the small beach in front of Rafe's house. I sit on the sand and I wait.

Where are you, Rafe? Come back to me.

I write another text. *I'm here in Malibu, waiting for you. Please come home. I love you.*

I sit there and watch the sunset.

When it's dark and there's still no sign of him, I go back up to the house. I go upstairs. I get undressed and get into his bed.

My tears wet his pillows.

Please come back to me.

29

———

RAFE

Holy hell.

Ow.

Fuck.

Fuck.

Fuck.

My head.

I need water.

I need water.

I need water.

It's getting dark.

I'm no longer drunk and this is a very bad thing. Clarity slices into my brain along with the merciless knife blades of my colossal hangover. I'm severely dehydrated and suffering from a savage case of the DTs.

I manage to stand up and it's a good thing there's nothing in my stomach or it would have come hurling out.

As it is, I manage to stumble down the small staircase and into the galley.

And there, on a shelf in the small kitchen: my salvation. Twelve wrapped bottles of spring water. I rip the packaging open and start guzzling that warm liquid like the lifeblood that it is, barely coming up for air until I've drunk four of the fuckers.

There's canned food here, too, and a can opener.

I'm starving. When's the last time I fucking ate something? I can't remember. I eat a couple of cans of caviar, then some instant stew, cold, with a spoon, right out of the can.

I even find some aspirin.

And I've made up my mind. I'm not having another drink for a very long time.

And I'm going after her.

Fuck boundaries. Fuck everything. What have I done that's so terrible, anyway? Knocked someone up, yes. *Unintentionally. Before* I even met her! What was I supposed to have done, *predicted* that she would walk into my life? Like a goddamn *psychic* or something? It isn't *my* fault that psychotic bitch sabotaged me.

So what if Vanessa's pregnant? It doesn't mean Lexi and I can't be together. I should *never* have listened to Lexi, there at the altar. I should never have let her walk away, pleads and demands or not. We'd all been a little overcome by the news, that's all. Now it's time to work it the fuck out.

Because I can't live without her. End of story. I don't *want* to live without her. Why should I have to? I can be a father to my child and still be a husband to the woman I love, even if the two aren't connected. People do that shit all the time!

Why hadn't I thought of all this before?

Because I was too drunk to process anything, possibly.

Well, I'm not drunk now. I have one bitch of a hangover but the aspirin is helping.

I check my pockets for my phone.

It's completely dead. Do I have a charger? A USB?

I can't find anything and I don't want to waste any more time. I'm going home. I'm going to win back my girl and I'm not taking no for an answer, that's all there is to it. I'll sling her over my shoulder, take her to bed and refuse to let her out of it until she listens to me. I'll win her back and convince her because it's the only thing I care about.

We love each other. We're meant to be together. That kind of thing just doesn't come along every day of the goddamn week and I'm not going to let anything get in the way of us. That baby can be part of us along with everything else in our lives. Bring it on.

I'm coming to find you, baby girl. Can you feel me?

Dusk gives way to night. There's no breeze at all, which means I either have to use the small motor on the boat, which isn't designed for long distances, or I'll have to wait it out until the wind picks up. I have no idea where the fuck I am.

Then I remember. The SAT phone.

I find it and turn it on. I realize I'd turn off all the communications systems somewhere in the middle of my drunken stupor. As I try to make contact, I see lights in the distance.

The SAT phone rings and I pick it up.

"Rafe Black?"

"Yes." My voice is hoarse from lack of use and dehydration.

"This is the Coast Guard. You're a hundred miles out at sea, Mr. Black. We've got you in our sights and we're taking you back in."

A hundred miles? Jesus. How long was I out for?

BY THE TIME I get back to the house, the first light of dawn is coloring the horizon a light shade of pink.

The house, as I walk into it, is quiet. The staff must have gone home.

But then I see something. A jacket, hung over the back of a chair. A lightweight one I bought her, made of black silk. I pick it up. I hold it to my face and inhale. I almost swoon from the scent of it. Of *her*.

She's here.

I go up the stairs. To my bedroom.

More of her clothes are draped over a chair. *All* of her clothes.

Her small form is in the bed, curled under the covers.

Her hair, spilling out, catches the moonlight in a glimmering glow.

Very gently, I peel back the covers.

She wakes, and her eyes widen. Pure relief colors her expression. And it's a look that's so full of love I can only stare.

"Rafe," she whispers, the sound of her voice slaying me. She opens her arms to me. "Oh, thank God you're here. I love you. I love you. Come here, Rafey. Let me feel you. I need you so much."

30

MY RAFE LOOKS DIFFERENT. Haunted. He's lost weight. His hair is wild. His skin is dark with sun and sunburn. He smells like moonlight and sea salt, with the slightest hint of whiskey. He's wearing a pair of worn shorts that are frayed at the edges, that hang low on his lean hips. He looks, in a word, *human*.

And more beautiful than ever before.

First, I send a text to Max. *He's home. He's here and he's safe. We'll call you a little later.* Max texts back immediately. *Thank u Lex* with a praying hands emoji and a heart.

Rafe is very quiet. He seems overcome. Dazed.

He slides into bed next to me.

I wrap my arms and my legs around him. I kiss his face. I bury my fingers in his hair. I kiss his mouth. Slow, careful kisses. Communicating my love for him. Kisses that turn slippery and lust-sweet. He lets me kiss him and I can feel in him the awe, which gives way to a hunger. Our hands are everywhere, slow and grasping. We can't hold each other close enough.

"You just can't do that to me, sweetheart," he murmurs. "I can't take it."

"There's no baby, Rafe."

He stares at me. His eyes are blue even in the darkness. "What?"

"Max and your lawyers convinced her to take a pregnancy test. It was negative."

"It was?"

"Yes."

"*Fuck.* Thank God. Thank *God.*"

I wonder if a part of him might be sad about it. "Are you okay?"

"Of course I'm okay. I'm more than okay. I'm over the fucking moon, honey. I want to have my babies with *you,* Lexi. *You.*"

The news seems to transform him and focus him. He's astoundingly hard, gripping me with his fingers.

"I need you," he rasps.

"Are you sure? You—"

"Now. Right now." His self-control seems to have vanished, replaced by raw emotion.

"Yes. It's okay. Be careful, Rafey." He grips me even more tightly, kneeing my legs apart, blindly finding his way inside. I'm wet but tight and he thrusts into me, driving deep until he's fully rooted. He sobs my name and I kiss him again, sucking softly on his tongue as I love him with everything I have. *I'll always love you,* I tell him. *We'll never be apart again.* He groans and loses himself, throbbing hotly inside me, filling me with gushes of his silky heat.

I kiss him for a long time, smoothing his hair, touching his face. I kiss his lips, his rough jaw. He needs a shave.

"Where did you go?" he says quietly.

"New York."

Shadowed circles under his eyes, like bruises, show his exhaustion. "Really? Why New York?"

"New York seemed like a place I could...get lost. Besides, I didn't want to go to Venice without you."

"Venice?"

"I want to go there one day."

"How about tomorrow?" The look in his eyes, of understanding and sorrow, of a love so profound I once thought it would break us both. Now I know better. "I was coming to find you."

"I was coming to find you, too," I whisper.

He kisses me again, his tongue dipping into my mouth in intimate plunges, until he's fully, immensely hard again. His hands grip me closer as his weight pins me down. His pace is deliberate and unrelenting. We ride the incremental rise as he thrusts into me, going deeper, forcing the pleasure higher. I gaze into his dark eyes, digging my fingernails into him. The climax is lush and brimming. I cry out as he growls my name and finds his own release.

We lay there, locked and entwined in a soul-touching embrace, my body still fluttering tightly around his deeply-insinuated bulk.

"Don't run from me again, honey. Please. I just can't handle it. Next time, I'm chasing after you, even if I have to wander the earth until my dying day."

"I'm done running, Rafe. I don't want to ever be apart from you again."

"Lex, will you marry me. Now? Today?"

"Guess what today is?" I ask him.

"What?"

"Today's my birthday."

He smiles, that heart-breaking smile. "We met on my birthday and we'll get married on yours. That's what I'm going to do, baby girl. I'm going to marry you on your birthday and make all your dreams come true."

And that's exactly what he does.

RAFE and I get married on my twenty-first birthday, barefoot on the beach in Malibu.

Max, after explaining everything to the judge—who seems to have taken a shine to him—is allowed to attend our second attempt at a wedding, as long as he's back home by his earlier curfew of midnight.

We don't bother with the other guests this time. It's just me and Rafe and Max and Tess and the Justice of the Peace.

My Vera Wang has a couple of feathers missing, but it still fits like a dream.

We take our vows and we have our first dance to a song Max plays on an old acoustic guitar he brought just for the occasion.

We drink champagne and watch the sun set over the

water as Tess cries and Max insists on a dance. We laugh and these people, I realize, are…my *family*.

It's a magical night.

Limos take Tess and Max back to their apartments and Rafe and I leave for Venice the very next morning.

We ride the gondolas through the canals of Venice and visit the museums. We eat pasta and drink wine. We make love and we fall deeper than I ever thought it was possible to do. I give up trying to shield myself or to hold back. I give him everything. I know I'll never leave him again. I'm careful with his scars and he's careful with mine. I can trust him. And so I let myself do exactly that.

Venice feels like *ours*.

After a week in Venice and a tour of Rome and then Tuscany, we head back to L.A. to resume our lives and jobs at Downtown. Eric Scully left of his own free will. He and Rafe even had a meeting about it and they seem to be on speaking terms again.

I work by Rafe's side most days, and he's getting (sort of) better at letting me out of his sight. *I like you* in *my sight,* is what he has to say about that and, after our time apart, I have to admit, I don't like letting him out of my sight either.

Rafe has fixed me, in so many ways. I like to think we've fixed each other.

Vanessa came to me and apologized in a dramatic,

tearful confession. She was so desperate to win him back she admits she acted rashly. I forgave her. I understand how hard it would be to let go of Rafe Black. Rafe, though, won't see her or speak to her. He thinks her lie was vicious, insane, and cost him three days of his life. I see it differently. The time we spent apart just cemented the fact that we'll always come back to each other, no matter what happens.

Either way, Vanessa lost her column and all ties to Downtown, but her career hasn't suffered. People love a story. I also heard she's now dating someone new. A GQ model, apparently, with dark hair and blue eyes.

Rafe asked me to create my dream job, and I have. It's a small department, but one that's growing quickly. It's called "Spotlight on L.A." and will showcase artists, writers, activists, fashion designers, filmmakers, politicians, and so on. People who are making their mark on the city's landscape in new and interesting ways. Tess is helping me. She does three days in the fashion department and two days with me. Her blog now has two million followers and she just bought herself a swanky little bungalow in West Hollywood.

Rafe continues to astound me every single day. Ours is a love story that began within a tsunami of lust. Something simply clicked in a way that changed us both and committed us irrevocably to each other before we could even question it. He is the most devoted lover, the most dedicated husband, the most beautiful, infuriating, affectionate, intelligent man I have ever met. I love him so much my heart sometimes feels like it's on the verge of breaking from the overflow.

I'm still on the pill, but I don't want to wait too long. I don't see the point in waiting for years to do something we both want sooner than that. On my twenty-second birthday, I'll tell him what I want and see what he thinks.

Max's home detention will finish soon. He wrote a heartfelt email to all his clients that convinced them he was, actually, innocent. Max just has this way about him that you can't help but believe whatever he says. I know *I* believe him and so does Rafe. Since he got arrested, he's thrown himself into his work with a new perspective and has somehow almost doubled the number of clients they're handling at the investment company he runs from his home office. Their revenue has skyrocketed. He said he's committed to keeping everything legit and he has a knack, so people are dying to work with him. It also doesn't hurt that he's drop-dead gorgeous. More than half their new clients are women.

But Max doesn't seem interested in any of them and in fact has been spending a lot of time at that restaurant in his zone.

Turns out that he's not a player anymore, not at all.

Once Max met the right girl, he fell *hard*. It's kind of adorable, the way he behaves with her. I'm just happy he found someone who can handle him. I'm a little surprised to see that he's just as possessive as Rafe, or—dare I say it —maybe even worse.

As for how that all unfolds, well, that's another story...

Thank you for reading! If you enjoyed Rafe and Lexi's story, please consider leaving a quick review or rating on Amazon for <u>XOXO I Love You</u> and <u>XOXX I Love You More</u>.

Below I've included a sneak peek of the brand new—and free—extended epilogue to the I Love You series, **Love You The Most**, which includes babies and an OTT steamy and romantic HEA! How many babies do you think Rafe and Lexi have? It's all revealed in their final epilogue.

I've also included Chapter One of **MAX**, a sexy standalone spin-off to the series. I fell in love with Max as I was writing this series and knew he needed his own HEA.

xoxo,

Julie

Please come join my Facebook reader group, Julie

Capulet's Romantics, where I share cover reveals, insider info and we discuss all things romance!

Sign up for my newsletter to receive my free bonus content and get access to sneak peeks and exclusive giveaways!

Visit my website @ www.juliecapulet.com

LOVE YOU THE MOST
Extended Epilogue to the I Love You Duet

~ Sneak Peek ~

"How does it feel to have stormed on to the scene so suddenly, like you have?" I'm interviewing Travis Tucker, the front man of a hot new country-rock band whose fourth album, like their other three, has hit number one on the Billboard charts. This is my role now at Downtown and has been for almost a year. I run my own features department, where I interview musicians, writers, movie stars and other movers and shakers. It's the job I chose and created, and I absolutely love it. And my best friend Tess works alongside me, as one of three fashion executive editors, which makes it even more fun.

"It feels fucking good," Travis drawls. He leans back in his chair, knees apart. His worn jeans and faded shirt show off his gracefully muscular physique. He's hot and he knows it. We're in my swanky, modern office and he looks out of place, with his windblown hair, his double denim, cowboy boots and his full-on Nashville vibe. He's so suntanned and outdoorsy-looking, he might as well have just stepped straight out of a corn field. His look is sort of wholesome meets bad boy. "But it doesn't feel all that sudden. My brothers and I have been writing songs and playing together since we were kids. Our overnight success has taken years of work, but we're glad the fans are enjoying the music. That's who we do it for."

The Tucker Brothers Band consists of Travis and his two brothers, Vaughn and Kade. All three of them are ridiculously good-looking. That, combined with their cool, artsy style and their obvious über-talent have skyrocketed them to the heights of fame and fortune over the course of a few short years. They also seem to be constantly surrounded by scandal after scandal, only upping their street appeal.

I check my list of questions. "Your first three albums sat more squarely in the country scene. How would you describe your new album?"

"Country, bluegrass, rockabilly, gospel, rock. It's all in there. Our inspiration isn't limited to one style of music. We like to mix it up. But, yeah, our new album is heavier. It's more rock 'n roll, I guess you could say."

"How are you handling the fame? Has it changed your life?"

"Completely. The crowds can get pretty rabid, but it's cool. We love our fans. I do miss peace and privacy occasionally. I'm thinking about buying a house out in the country. I'll starting looking around soon to see what I can find. I thought it might be nice to have a private, peaceful getaway. Our life on the road can get pretty hectic."

"I suppose you can't tell us where you're looking for your new getaway house?"

He grins. I'm sure it's a smile that's left a trail of broken hearts across America and beyond. "That would sort of defeat the purpose, now, wouldn't it? But maybe for you, I could make an exception."

I smile back at him, but I glide right past his comment. "Your latest national tour sold out within ten minutes. Will you add more shows?"

"We already have." Travis winks at me, then his gaze lands on my wedding ring. It's the only ring I usually wear. My engagement ring is too big and ostentatious to wear every day. People tend to stare, not surprisingly. All the other rings Rafe bought me are sitting with my Tiffany engagement ring, in a special drawer, still in their jewelry store boxes. They're all so incredibly over-the-top, they loudly announce to everyone I meet that I have a very rich husband. Which isn't always the first detail about myself I want to advertise. This frustrates him to no end, but he knows I like to do things my own way. He's still adjusting and learning to live with that. "We're playing a few smaller venues as we tour," Travis continues, "which we actually prefer to the stadiums. It's more intimate." At the word *intimate*, he looks right at me. He's got one of those proverbial twinkles in his very-green eyes. "You should come to the one in L.A. tomorrow night. It's at an undisclosed location."

I didn't hear the door open, but I suddenly sense his unmistakable squally, brooding presence.

Rafe.

His hand rests possessively on my shoulder and he leans down to kiss my neck. "Hey, baby," he murmurs and I can smell his scent. Spiced man-scent, so purely Rafe.

Travis stands to shake Rafe's hand. "Travis Tucker." He's grinning, like he's amused by the fact that he was on the verge of propositioning me. He obviously doesn't know Rafe—or what he's capable of.

"Rafe Black."

They shake hands briefly and Rafe stays close to me, half-sitting against my desk. It's not unusual for him to drop in unexpectedly. He does it all the time. He wanted to share an office at first, but I refused. Then he insisted I take the office next to his, an arrangement we tried for a month before I decided it wasn't working out very well. We distract each other. We ended up having sex...*a lot*, to the point where people were starting to get suspicious about why our doors were locked all the time. And why we weren't actually getting any work done.

So I moved to the corner office that's on the other side of the building. It's the only way I can work.

That doesn't stop him from checking up on me many times a day. Or, as he puts it, needing to get his fix. I don't mind, of course. I need my fix as much as he does. Our relationship started out as something close to an addiction to each other, a lust that overwhelmed us both. Now, it's mellowed somewhat, but it's still...intense. He's my husband, my lover, my best friend and my favorite person. I love him with a deep, complicated passion I didn't even know I was capable of. He's the love of my life. To say he feels the same way would be an understatement.

And now that Rafe has seen Travis, there's no way in hell he's leaving.

Even after a year of marriage, he still takes my breath away. His thick black hair, smoothed into place, curls at the edge of his collar. He needs a haircut. His tall, beautiful form, burly arms folded across his broad chest. His darkly perceptive blue eyes watching me. Studying the vibe of the room. His jealousy is already on overdrive, I can feel that. Rafe doesn't like other men to even *look* at me, let alone check me out, or whatever Travis is doing. Whatever it is, it's mild. He's a down-home boy, it's not usually his style to go after married women and he probably wouldn't act on it. That's my guess.

Either way, Rafe isn't pleased.

Travis's phone pings in his back pocket. Maybe he

senses Rafe's storm cloud. "That's my manager, who also happens to be my sister. She'll have my head on a plate if I don't stick to the schedule." Travis's tone takes on a respectful but amused air. "Lexi, it was a pleasure. And I meant it about those tickets. If the two of you would like to come along tomorrow night, I'll let the door people know to expect you."

"We're busy," says Rafe. "But thanks."

But I'm used to Rafe. I know how to handle him. "Actually, Travis, we'd love two tickets. Thank you so much. I've always wanted to see your band. I love your music. I've been listening to you since you first released your first album."

Travis glances at Rafe, his eyebrow slightly raised, like he's entertained by Rafe's bullish he-man shtick and is wondering if he might go full caveman. Rafe stays silent. Travis grins and says, "All right, then. I'll try to come and say hi. Sometimes things get crazy, especially if word gets out. Either way, enjoy the show."

"Thanks for taking the time to come by today, Travis. I know how busy you must be."

"It's no problem at all." To Rafe, "Nice to meet you, man."

"Likewise." Glaring. Like a man-eating lion on the savannah whose territory has been encroached on.

Exhaling a light laugh, Travis leaves, closing the door behind him.

Rafe stands there, fuming. Looking gorgeous. More than gorgeous. *Delicious.* He's the most beautiful man I've ever seen. I still can't believe he's mine.

"You're dreaming if you think I'm going to sit there for hours watching you drool all over those fucking redneck brothers," he says gruffly.

I can't help smiling at him. "Oh, we're going to the concert. Because they're good and because I want to see them. But I won't be drooling all over *them*." I loosen the knot at my waist that holds my silk wraparound dress together. I stand close to him, on my toes so I can kiss his lips. I let my dress fall open. "I'll be drooling all over my hot, grouchy, jealous-for-no-reason husband."

His breath catches. "You interviewed him like *that*? No wonder he was practically jumping you when I walked in."

I laugh and touch my lips to his.

I'm not wearing anything under my dress, something Rafe likes me to do when we're alone. I only did it today because I knew I'd be spending the afternoon with him. Today happens to be my birthday so I didn't overdo my work schedule. Travis was my only interview of the day.

I brush my naked breasts against Rafe's expensive suit, touching my tongue to his succulent lower lip. "*He* didn't know I wasn't wearing anything underneath. This is for you, Rafe. Always you. Only you."

I love this man so much it hurts. I love him more than I knew I was capable of loving anyone. I love that he's at my mercy, like I'm at his mercy. I pull on his tie and lead him over to my leather office couch. I love that he's so big and powerful but that he obeys me because he has no choice. And I love that he wants me so much it sometimes—okay, *always*—makes him insane with lust and love and possessiveness. I gently push him so he's sitting. And I let my dress fall to the floor. All I'm wearing is my high heeled boots, a small pair of gold hoop earrings and my wedding ring.

"I want my birthday present now," I tell him. Today is my 22nd birthday. I married Rafe on my 21st.

"I already gave you your present." This morning before I even got out of bed he gave me a tennis bracelet made entirely of rubies, a new jet ski that's at our house in Hawaii, the latest iPhone, two dozen white roses...and three orgasms. So far.

"I want more." I unfasten his pants, freeing his big cock, which is already rock hard. He's huge and silky and beautifully made, like a living sculpture. I can never get enough of his dazzling male beauty. There's too much of it to ever get used to. He astounds me with it every single day. "I have a secret I've been keeping from you," I tell him as I climb onto him, touching the leaking head of his cock with my fingertips, guiding him closer. Of course I'm wet for him. I felt the secret heat the minute his lips kissed my neck and I smelled his scent.

We have this effect on each other. A year of marriage

has done nothing to tone it down. If anything, our deepening love has only stoked the passion higher.

"What secret?" His eyes are dark sapphires. Rafe hates secrets. He wants to know everything. Every thought, every wish.

I rub his big cock against my wet pussy and he holds my hips in place. He thrusts into me as I sink lower. The stretching slide of his thickness makes me gasp and he thrusts again until I'm seated onto him, fully impaled. I squeeze him gently with my body as I kiss his perfect lips. "I went to see my doctor yesterday."

He goes still. "Why? Is something wrong?"

"Nothing's wrong. Everything's fine. I went to talk to her about going off the pill."

Rafe's been wanting me to go off the pill for a while. He just turned 28. We had a scare last year involving an ex-girlfriend of his who he broke up with before he met me. *Scare* is actually putting it mildly. It temporarily derailed our entire wedding and caused us to postpone it for several weeks, but we worked it out.

It was a horrible time, being apart from him, but it taught me that I don't want to live without Rafe. It forged our bond even more deeply. We were so lost without each other that it made us appreciate each other in a way that has shaped our relationship ever since. We're careful with each other. We're wildly grateful the other one exists, complexities and all. We're so in tune with our love for each other that we celebrate it and act on it deeply, and in a way I think might be unusual. I can't be sure about that. All I know is that I love my husband with my whole heart.

Ever since the wedding fiasco happened, Rafe talks about having babies all the time. I think he's so relieved that *his* babies will be *our* babies, he wants to get on with it. He said he's ready whenever I am, but he's prepared to be as patient as he needs to be, since I'm still young.

Lately my feelings have changed on that topic. I *do* feel ready. I don't want to wait too much longer. I want to have babies with my dream man. I'm so incredibly lucky and I appreciate that luck every day. I don't want to waste any of it. I want to act on it and fully *live*.

Lately I've been thinking about what our babies will look like. What we might name them. Who they'll take after. And how Rafe will be as a father. Never having had a father in my own life at all, it fills me with overwhelming love for my husband, just at the thought. My babies are going to have the most protective, attentive, dedicated, amazing father in the world.

Rafe seems overcome by my announcement. "You *did*?" I can feel his cock rear up and harden even more inside me, like he's rising to the challenge. He holds my face in his warm hands. "Are you sure, honey?"

"The doctor said I'm healthy and there's no reason not to start trying, if you want to. So I didn't take my pill this morning. I'll stop taking it, if you want to...you know, start trying."

The dark blue fever in his eyes burns even hotter and even more brightly than usual. "Of course I do, sweetheart. I want that more than anything. I've been wanting that all along." I guess it's safe to say that he's ready...

Get your FREE copy to continue reading!
@ juliecapulet.com/bonuscontent

I notice him as soon as he walks into my chic new Los Angeles restaurant. Of course I do. He's tall and built, with tattoos and a dark, pirate-king vibe. According to rumors, he's also an investment genius who happens to be a billionaire.

But this is no fairy tale. He's wearing one of those criminal cuffs on one wrist and a Rolex on the other.

Just what I don't need. A rich bad boy with rage issues. It's scary enough that one of my customers has been stalking me.

But when the stalker follows me home one night, it's Max who saves me—the gorgeous blue-eyed stranger who could be either the devil or a saint.

He's dangerous, but I've never felt so safe. He's a sinner who saves me in every possible way. He becomes my haven, my protector, my paradox.

And he's the love story I never saw coming...

Max is a spin-off from the I Love You series and is a sexy standalone story.

Chapter One

I've held back my rage for a long time but today I feel like pummeling someone—anyone—into next goddamn week. When I find out who screwed me over...I just hope I can control myself long enough not to kill the fucker and end up in a goddamn jail cell. Then again, getting convicted for a crime I actually *did* commit might be a whole lot more satisfying than getting burned for one I didn't.

I walk through the door of my penthouse office and shut the door. What I feel like doing is slamming it, smashing the place up and hunting down the asshole who put me in this mess. But those days are long gone. I'm not an amped-up punk anymore. I'm a level-headed overachiever with an Ivy League degree under my belt, five luxury properties to my name and a net worth of more than four hundred million dollars. I am—*was*, until earlier this afternoon—CFO of a Fortune 500 investment company and Chairman of the Goddamn Board of Directors.

I make a point of keeping my cool.

Barely.

I run a hand through my hair. I need a haircut. Hell, maybe I won't even bother. I won't be seeing the inside of a boardroom anytime soon. I stuff my $5,000 Armani jacket into one of the cardboard boxes now sitting in my office. Usually I don't show my tats at work but who gives a fuck? Today it doesn't matter. I roll up my sleeves and yank off my tie. My shirt feels too tight, possibly because I've been working out like a goddamn maniac lately. I start packing a few things from the shelves into the boxes.

My phone rings.

I almost don't answer it, but my brother's name flashes up on the screen. We have a deal: we always answer. No matter how shitty our day might've been. And today pretty much takes the cake.

Rafe launches straight into it. "Home detention's no reason to bail on me. Come out to dinner with us tonight."

"No. I'll see you tomorrow."

"Max," he says. "I'm getting *married* in two days. I need my best man there tonight to help me celebrate. Besides,

Lexi found a place that's right around the corner from your office. We're heading down there now to meet Lexi's maid of honor, Tess. You met her the other night."

I got convicted of insider trading today and my brother bailed me out on the spot. Instead of a jail sentence, I'll be serving a three-month stint of home detention. I've been fitted with an electronic bracelet which, if I happen to step outside my jurisdiction, will blow my fucking head off. Okay, maybe it won't. But it might as well. I've been ordered by the judge not to leave the three-block square where my apartment and my office are located. I can walk between the two, or drive my Ducati, or any of the other six cars or twelve motorcycles parked in my private garage. If I get caught outside the zone I'll get thrown in jail for at least three years with no possibility of parole. I've also been "asked" by the Board of Directors to take a break from my job as CFO of my brother's largest investment company.

I don't really feel like dinner but, hell, I owe him one. In fact I owe him a lot more than one. Six fucking million, to be exact. "Shit. All right," I say.

The only reason I'm agreeing to meet my brother and his fiancée is because they're about to get married. I want to see them. But I wish it could be the three of us and not a foursome with some over-eager friend who's guaranteed to drool over me all night. I'm really not in the mood.

I haven't been in the mood for a while.

"I didn't do it, by the way," I say. "And I'll deposit the six mil into your Bahamas account later tonight."

"Didn't do what?"

"Leak the info."

"What do you mean?"

"I mean someone framed me." I could have told him before but there was no point. There's zero evidence to back up my claims. A stack of emails written from my private account was presented to the court, making an airtight case against me. "Someone hacked into my account and sent the emails. I didn't give out any insider information. I'm clean as a goddamn whistle."

Rafe's silent for a couple of seconds, like he can't believe what he's hearing. "Why didn't you tell me this?"

"Because I knew I didn't stand a chance in court. And I didn't want to draw it out." I have a long list of criminal offenses. Mostly minor shit I did when I was younger. Even though I've spent the past ten years trying to make up for all that by working my ass off and heading several major companies, I have enough of a record to skew any judge's opinion of me in the wrong direction. I know what I look like to a judge: a badass. A shady delinquent with a history. The kind of guy the law has a problem with.

Rafe knows all this.

"I have a few ideas about who might've framed me," I tell him, "but there's no point naming names until I have proof."

"You should've told me," Rafe says again.

"I didn't want it to look like we were trying to cover something up. Then the whole company looks dirty. This way, it's just me."

"Jesus, Max."

When you're dealing with the kind of money we throw around on a daily basis, it's dog-eat-dog, everyone knows that. I earn ten million dollars a year working for my brother, plus commission, which is usually double my salary, and sometimes more. Everyone who works with me wants my job and they all think the only reason I'm there is because my brother owns the company. Which used to be true. Not anymore. I'm good at building companies and I'm good at making money. It took me a while to get on track in life but these days I can spot a winner from a mile away.

"Until then," I add, "I'll be taking a little hiatus from the office."

"I own the damn company, Max. If you want to stay you can stay."

"I can still advise the brokers from my home office. Don't sweat it. I need a break anyway."

"I'll fucking slam whoever did this."

"Yeah, you and me both."

"I'll call an investigator I use," Rafe says. "We'll get to the bottom of this."

Taking time out from my job doesn't worry me. Letting my brother down does. Those days are over.

His sigh is pissed-off. "At least let me buy you a drink."

"Fine, then. I'll see you in twenty." I end the call and set the phone on my desk, which is strewn with court orders and legal documents. Irate letters from clients questioning my ethics and calling for my dismissal.

I'll clear my name if it's the last thing I do. I swore a long time ago I'd never get another criminal conviction, so this one stings a lot more than I'd like to admit.

I pick up a pink envelope from my stack of mail. *Another one?* Hell, she just won't quit. I get a lot of cards and letters from women. This one is from a girl I had dinner around six months ago. Or was it longer than that? I met her at a charity function, I remember that much. I'd donated a lot of money to a charity that helps down-and-out teens get into college. I *was* a down-and-out teen once so I understand how much of a difference the help of one person can make. So they sent me a free ticket to the event and I'd ended up going. She saw me from across the room and confessed she moved the seating arrangement so she could sit next to me. This happens to me all the time so I didn't think much of it. The conversation had been almost entirely one-sided. She drank a lot and asked me back to her place. Even though she was sending all the wrong signals—overly needy, borderline stalkerish, the kind of woman who clings when it's the very last thing you want them to do—I'd taken her home.

A terrible decision, as it turned out, like so many are.

It had played out the way it always does. For me, it was unfulfilling because no emotion or genuine interest was involved at all. She'd told me it was the best sex of her life, begged me to stay, then had a dramatic meltdown when I tried to leave. I hadn't called or given her my number but she knows where I work and keeps sending me letters about how I broke her goddamn heart. I had to tell the door people to stop her from entering the building after she stormed up to my office once when I was in the middle of a meeting, crying and telling me she loves me.

After *one* night. Which is crazy.

Even so, it happens all the time. Go figure.

I'm probably the least lovable person I know. I'm broken, and unfixable.

I rip open the envelope.

Max, please call me. Please!!! I need to see you one more time. I know I'll be able to change your mind. I just want to talk to you. We're meant to be together. It's destiny, I can feel it. Please let me show you how much you mean to me. Please, Max. Call me back. All my love, Melanie.

I toss the card into the shredder.

I've tried to feel that spark. I *want* to feel that spark. The one that means you're supposed to be with someone for more than one night. Maybe even for—I don't know—a *month*, maybe. Or even a whole goddamn lifetime. People *do* that shit.

The problem is, I never feel that spark and I always end up regretting everything.

So I made a decision. Probably around six months ago. Soon after Melanie, as it turns out. I decided to take a break. It's the reason I've been pumping iron like it's going out of style. All that pent up energy has to be spent somehow.

My pent up energy is on overdrive at this point. I feel like I'm about to fucking spontaneously combust.

And I'm getting tired of being alone.

It's possibly what I deserve, after the way I've treated women. Dismissive. Disengaged. Non-committal to the extreme. They accuse me of using them, then walking away. Which is true enough.

Anyway, there's no point crying about it but I'm a lost cause as far as relationships go. I came to terms with all that a long time ago.

I leave a note for my assistants to finish packing up my stuff and have it sent to my apartment. I close up my office and grab my worn black leather jacket. I walk down to the street. It's a warm night for October. There are a lot of people strolling around.

Even women who are arm-in-arm with their boyfriends or husbands check me out as I walk past.

I don't get it.

Women love me, for some reason.

Love me.

I don't dwell on it but it's just one of those things.

I've sometimes wondered what it is about me they're so desperate to have. They seem to love my looks, for better or for worse. I'm built. I'm tall. And I have an edge, which is roughly equivalent to crack for women, fuck knows why.

They even wanted me before I had money. Now, they're practically rabid.

Maybe I have the aura of someone who can do things to them no one else will. Or take them past some pleasure threshold no one else can. Who knows. Whatever it is, they watch me. They call me and pursue me relentlessly, which, lately, I've been doing my best to avoid.

I know what all this sounds like: I'm ungrateful or I'm an arrogant prick.

Not exactly.

I catch up to Rafe and Lexi just as Lexi's friend Tess is arriving, as they're walking into the restaurant. Rafe slings his arm around me like he's happy to see me. He's always happy to see me. We have the kind of bond a lot of brothers don't have. We've been through a lot together, me and him, and we know we've got each other's backs. The truth is, he's bailed me out more times than I can count but I feel like that'll start to change.

Lexi gives me a hug. My brother's fiancée is a catch, no doubt about it. She's gorgeous and is one of the nicest people I've ever met. "Hey, sweetheart," I say as she kisses my cheek. I laugh when Rafe eyeballs me. He's got some control issues when it comes to Lexi but we're cool.

The friend, Tess, who I've met once before, does what they all do: checks me out. Stares. First at my face then my body. She moves to step forward but I read her intention and take a step back before she even notices. It's something I'm well-practiced at. I don't like to be touched.

"Thanks for venturing into my jurisdiction," I say.

"For you?" Tess blushes. "Anything."

I return the smile but I'm so not in the mood for this. My muscles are clenched for no particular reason. Possibly because I'm still wound up from getting convicted of a federal offense a few hours ago and escaping a prolonged prison sentence by the skin of my goddamn teeth and six million dollars.

"Tess, let's go sit down," Lexi says, thankfully steering Tess away. I exhale, releasing a minuscule shred of the ocean of tension and despair that hounds me.

We walk further into the restaurant. "This place is so cute," Tess says.

I guess it is. It's got a lot of exposed brick and wood and mirrors. The ceiling's been decorated with yellow fairy lights and hanging bulbs, giving the place a festive atmosphere. And it's busy. I have no doubt Rafe would've thrown plenty of money around to get us the prime table by the window.

I take off my leather jacket and slide into my seat. The hostess appears and says something about getting us drinks. The bell-like tone of her voice makes me look up.

Her hair is strawberry-blond, a warm, golden color with fiery copper highlights.

Her face is angelic. More than that. Exquisite. She's cute but also gorgeous. She radiates a sweet, dazzling glow that is quite literally lighting up the room.

I realize I'm staring.

She's waiting for me and her expression is intrigued but slightly hassled. They're busy tonight and I'm holding her up. She has other things to do besides stand here and wait for me.

But I take my time. I can't help it. I want to watch her a little more. Check out the soft, bright colors of her. The deep blue shade of her eyes and her long eyelashes that blink at me as she waits. The sprinkling of freckles across her nose reminds me of summer. The mesmerizing pinkness of her lips and her pale, clear skin is fascinating me.

I'm stunned. More than that. I'm slayed.

I want to spend some time just watching her and drinking in every detail.

This is not something that's ever happened to me before.

But I can't pull my eyes away.

She's slim but curvy in all the right places. *Damn. All the right places.* Maybe I've just gone too long without and

I'm suddenly suffering the hellish consequences of my self-imposed monk-like existence. My chest feels tight and my heart's pumping fast. She's so fucking *beautiful.* My cock—*fuck*—goes instantly rock hard.

Damn it.

Max. Calm the fuck down.

The combination of her glow and her sweet, hot, completely-unaware-of-it cuteness quite literally hits me like a ton of bricks.

I won't act on it. Of course I won't. I'm a guy who ruins people's lives. A loose cannon, they call me. A rebel who never toes the line. A guy who uses women and breaks their hearts.

She's way too pure for the likes of me.

I'd dirty her with all my darkness. I'd rain all over her glowing sunny day.

I can't help fantasizing, though, just for a minute. What would it be like? To ask her out? On a real date. I honestly don't know if I've ever been on one.

I try to picture it. A wholesome, glorious, strawberry blond, blue-eyed, spectacularly dazzling date.

Or maybe two.

Or ten.

Ten thousand.

Ten fucking million, all strung together so there's no separation between them.

Fuck.

ALSO BY JULIE CAPULET

I Love You Series

The Obsession Begins (free)

XOXO I Love You

XOXX I Love You More

Love You The Most (free)

Sexy Standalones

Max

Cowboy

McCabe Brothers Series

Hopeless Romantic

My Hero

Arrogant Player

Music City Lovers Series

Nashville Days

Nashville Nights

Nashville Dreams

Nashville Lights

Hawthorne U Series

Lovestruck

Paradise Series

Devil's Angel

Wild Hearts

New York Billionaires Series

Billionaire Boss

Billionaire Grump

Billionaire Devil

Billionaire Romantic

Standalone Rom-com

Beautiful Savages

ABOUT THE AUTHOR

Julie Capulet is an Amazon top 20 bestselling author of contemporary romance. She writes steamy he-falls-first romance with heart, heat and fairy tale HEAs. Her stories are inspired by true love and she's married to her own real life hero. When she's not writing, she's reading, traveling, walking on the beach and watching rom-coms.

www.juliecapulet.com